DISNEYLAND CHALLENGE

DISNEY EDITIONS

NEW YORK

Written by Jim Fanning

The following are trademarks, registered marks, and service marks owned by Disney Enterprises, Inc.: Adventureland® Area Audio-Animatronics® Figures, Big Thunder Mountain Railroad, California Screamin', Circle-Vision, Critter Country, Disneyland® Park, Disneyland® Resort, Disney's California Adventure® Park, Downtown Disney® District, Fantasyland® Area, Frontierland® Area, Golden State®, Imagineering, Imagineers, "it's a small world," It's Tough To Be A Bug!® Attraction, Magic Kingdom® Park, Main Street, U.S.A.® Area, Mickey's Toontown®, monorail, New Orleans Square®, Paradise Pier®, Space Mountain® Attraction, Splash Mountain® Attraction, Tomorrowland® Area, Walt Disney World® Resort.

A Bug's Life; Finding Nemo; Monsters, Inc.; and Toy Story characters © Disney Enterprises, Inc. and Pixar Animation Studios

ESPN Zone © ESPN

Indiana Jones™ Adventure and Star Tours © Disney/Lucasfilm, Ltd.

© The Muppets Studio, LLC. GONZO, MISS PIGGY, KERMIT, FOZZIE BEAR and DR. BUNSEN HONEYDEW are trademarks of The Muppets Studio, LLC.

Roger Rabbit characters © Disney/Amblin

Tarzan's Treehouse® is a registered trademark of Edgar Rice Burroughs, Inc. All Rights Reserved.

The Twilight Zone is a registered trademark of CBS, Inc., and is used pursuant to a license from CBS, Inc.

Winnie the Pooh characters based on the "Winnie the Pooh" works by A. A. Milne and E. H. Shepard

Academy Award® and Oscar® are registered trademarks of the Academy of Motion Picture Arts and Sciences.

Attractions included within were operating at the time of the publication of the book.

For Disney Editions
Editorial Director: Wendy Lefkon
Senior Editor: Jody Revenson
Senior Designer: Tim Palin

Printed in Malaysia

ISBN: 978-14231-0675-3

The Official Community for Disney Fans
Disney.com/D23

HOW TO USE THIS BOOK

Whether this is your first or your fiftieth time in Disneyland Resort, there are always new surprises, secrets, and details being added to Disneyland Park and Disney's California Adventure Park to discover and enjoy. *Disneyland Challenge* will send you on great quests and captivating adventures, informing you of the attractions' and lands' histories, testing your Disney knowledge, and directing you to creative details that will enrich your time in the parks. Here are some samples of the categories you'll encounter in this book.

LOOK OUT!
There's something interesting here to see.

EARS TO YOU
There's something interesting here to hear.

SCAVENGER HUNT
Can you be the first to spot an interesting detail? Learn about its history at the same time.

SECOND TIME AROUND
Have you been there and done that? Here's a new way of seeing an attraction after you've been on it more than once.

QUEUE VIEWS
There's something of interest to see or do while waiting in the queue, and sometimes there's a challenge to pursue.

WHAT USED TO BE
Many attractions have changed since the Park's opening in 1955. Find out their fascinating histories.

WALT WAS HERE
Take note of an attraction that had Walt's personal attention.

BY THE NUMBERS
Count on this category to give you some statistical info.

ASK A CAST MEMBER.

CHALLENGE!
HOW MUCH DO YOU REALLY KNOW ABOUT THE PARK AND ITS ATTRACTIONS? THESE CHALLENGES WILL TEST YOUR KNOWLEDGE. THE ANSWERS FOR SOME CAN BE EASILY FOUND IN THE PARK. FOR OTHERS, IT MIGHT BE FUN TO GUESS — SEE WHO COMES CLOSEST OR HAS THE MOST ORIGINAL RESPONSE.

CHALLENGE YOURSELF!
These challenges are designed to enhance your experience through a physical action that might conclude with a surprising result. Here's one favorite: as you journey through the Park, hiss or boo whenever you see a Disney villain, such as Captain Hook, the Evil Queen, Jafar, or Cruella De Vil, as they walk down the street or in a parade. They don't expect that sort of challenge!

DISNEYLAND PARK

"I ONLY HOPE THAT WE NEVER LOSE SIGHT OF ONE THING," SAID WALT DISNEY, "THAT IT WAS ALL STARTED BY A MOUSE."

DISNEYLAND PARK OPENED ON JULY 17, 1955, AND HAS WELCOMED MORE THAN 500 MILLION GUESTS INTO ITS VARIOUS LANDS AND ON TO FUN, THRILLING, HUMOROUS, OR ADVENTUROUS ATTRACTIONS. INSIDE THE GATES OF DISNEYLAND IS ONE OF THE MOST PHOTOGRAPHED ICONS IN THE "HAPPIEST PLACE ON EARTH"—THE CHARMING FLORAL "DRAWING" OF MICKEY MOUSE WITH THE EAR-TO-EAR SMILE.

They've been dying to meet you at the

Haunted Mansion

...fying sight and sound!
...LEANS SQUARE

LOOK OUT!

In each "land" of Disneyland, you will find everything designed to fit that area's theme. Look for the specially created trash cans in each land—colored and styled to match their environments.

ASK A CAST MEMBER

Main Street, U.S.A., is a great place to start meeting and greeting your favorite Disney friends. Ask a Cast Member when and where the Fab Five will be for a hello and an autograph. Can you name the Fab Five?

Mickey Mouse, Minnie Mouse, Donald Duck, Goofy, and Pluto. Add Daisy Duck, and you have a stupendous six!

When they're not in a parade or a show, the Princesses (often with their Princes) appear in different lands, as do other friends from the Disney animated and live-action films. You can wish Alice and the Mad Hatter a merry unbirthday, or suggest some wishes for the Genie to grant you. You never know who's going to walk around the next corner! Most Cast Members have a "hotline" to their next appearance.

CHALLENGE! WHAT WAS WALT'S ORIGINAL NAME FOR DISNEYLAND?

Mickey Mouse Park

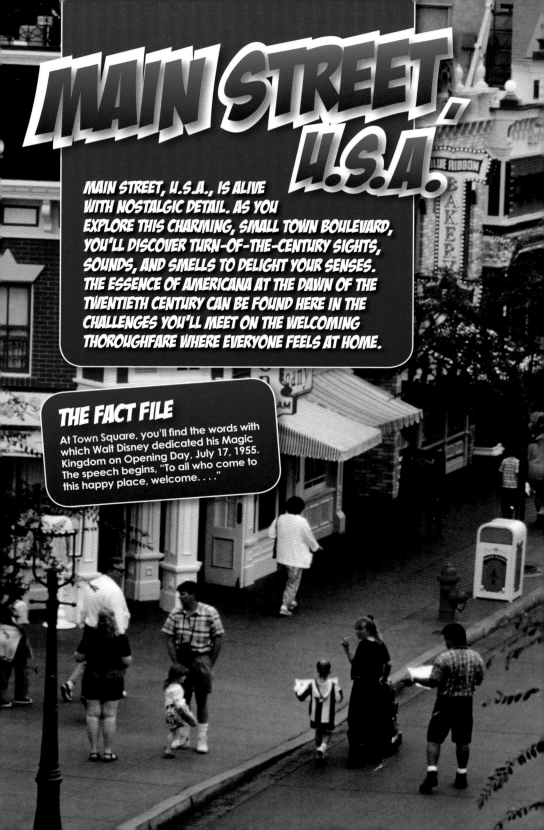

MAIN STREET, U.S.A.

MAIN STREET, U.S.A., IS ALIVE WITH NOSTALGIC DETAIL. AS YOU EXPLORE THIS CHARMING, SMALL TOWN BOULEVARD, YOU'LL DISCOVER TURN-OF-THE-CENTURY SIGHTS, SOUNDS, AND SMELLS TO DELIGHT YOUR SENSES. THE ESSENCE OF AMERICANA AT THE DAWN OF THE TWENTIETH CENTURY CAN BE FOUND HERE IN THE CHALLENGES YOU'LL MEET ON THE WELCOMING THOROUGHFARE WHERE EVERYONE FEELS AT HOME.

THE FACT FILE

At Town Square, you'll find the words with which Walt Disney dedicated his Magic Kingdom on Opening Day, July 17, 1955. The speech begins, "To all who come to this happy place, welcome. . . ."

CHECK IT OUT!

Above the Fire Department is an apartment Walt used during the building of Disneyland. The lamp in the window is always lit in his honor.

The Main Street lamps are originally from Baltimore, Maryland, and are lit by gas. They're each more than 150 years old and were bought for $ .03 a pound.

The cannons in Town Square were used by the French army in the nineteenth century, but they were never fired in battle.

Through the use of forced perspective, the Walt Disney Imagineers designed Main Street, U.S.A., to seem larger than it really is, giving it a charming, nostalgic atmosphere. The ground floors are about 7/8 scale with the second story at 5/8 scale and the third floor only half size.

Who's the lovely fortune-teller at the Arcade? Esmeralda has been in the Penny Arcade since Disneyland Park's Opening Day, so she knows about the past as well as your future.

CHALLENGE!

WHAT WAS THE FIRST BUILDING BUILT AT DISNEYLAND?

The Main Street Opera House. It served as the Park's lumber mill from 1955 to 1961.

WHAT IS THE DISNEYLAND BAND'S MOST-REQUESTED SONG?

The "Mickey Mouse March."

WHAT IS THE NUMBER OF THE FIRE STATION'S ENGINE COMPANY?

105

GETTING AROUND MAIN STREET

THERE ARE MANY WAYS TO GO FROM ONE END OF MAIN STREET TO THE OTHER, AS WELL AS TO CIRCLE THE PERIMETER OF THE PARK. HAVE YOU TRIED THEM ALL?

THE FACT FILE

The horses that pull Main Street's Horse-Drawn Streetcars are mostly Percheron draft horses and Belgians (known for their white manes and tails and lightly feathered legs). Clydesdales are also used at times. The horses have individual water fountains, custom-made suits, and a private beauty shop!

Added to the Disneyland Railroad in 1958, the Grand Canyon Diorama is a spectacular view of scenery as seen from the South Rim.

In 1966, Primeval World debuted to showcase the Audio-Animatronics dinosaur figures from the Ford Magic Skyway in the 1964–65 New York World's Fair.

DISNEYLAND RAILROAD

THE DISNEYLAND RAILROAD HAS BEEN EMBARKING ON A GRAND CIRCLE TOUR OF THE MAGIC KINGDOM SINCE OPENING DAY. FOUR OF THE FIVE TRAIN ENGINES WERE NAMED AFTER EXECUTIVES OF THE SANTA FE RAILROAD, THE ORIGINAL SPONSOR OF THE DISNEYLAND RAILROAD. (THE *WARD KIMBALL* IS NAMED AFTER AN ANIMATOR!)

CHALLENGE!

WHAT ARE THE OTHER FORMS OF TRANSPORTATION?

Double-decker Omnibuses, horse-drawn turn-of-the-nineteenth-century streetcars, and motorized jalopies

NAME THE ANIMALS YOU SEE IN THE GRAND CANYON DIORAMA.

Deer, mountain lion, desert mountain sheep, golden eagle, wild turkeys, porcupines, and skunks

NAME THE DINOSAURS IN PRIMEVAL WORLD.

Brontosaurus, stegosaurus, Tyrannosaurus rex, triceratops, pteranodons (munching on the plants), edaphosaurus (with fin shapes on their backs), ornithomimuses (the ostrich-looking ones)

SHOPS, SIGHTS, AND SOUNDS ON MAIN STREET

WHAT WOULD A STROLL DOWN MAIN STREET, U.S.A., BE WITHOUT A LITTLE WINDOW-SHOPPING? WITH OLD-FASHIONED WARES, SWEET TREATS, AND ELEGANT TREASURES, THE MANY QUAINT STORES OFFER A CORNUCOPIA OF BROWSING DELIGHTS.

CHALLENGE!

WHO ARE THE CHARACTERS AROUND THE "PARTNERS" STATUE?

Goofy, Dumbo, Pinocchio, Minnie, Donald Duck, Chip & Dale, White Rabbit

CHECK IT OUT!

As you stroll down Main Street, look up at the windows on the second floor. Made-up businesses honor Walt's family and the many Imagineers and Cast Members who helped design and enhance Disneyland through the decades.

CHECK IT OUT!

When the Park opened in 1955, its "hub and spoke" design was a revolutionary concept. Walt realized that a Central Plaza would help guests to easily enter or cross over to any of the four original "lands" of Disneyland. At the center of the Hub is a bronze statue of Walt and Mickey Mouse, called "Partners," which was dedicated on November 18, 1993, to commemorate Mickey's sixty-fifth birthday.

EARS TO YOU

Find the Hotel Marceline above the Market House and listen carefully—you may hear hotel guests talking.

Be sure to pick up a receiver on one of the many old-fashioned crank telephones hanging on the Market House walls. You can listen in on an 1890 party-line conversation.

CHALLENGE!

WHAT IS THE SHAPE OF MOST OF THE MAIN STREET HITCHING POSTS?

A horse's head

WHERE IS THE HITCHING POST THAT LOOKS LIKE IT WAS MADE FROM A TREE TRUNK?

Outside the China Closet shop

ADVENTURELAND

IN ADVENTURELAND, EXCITING CHALLENGES LURK EVERYWHERE. ONE QUICK TURN CAN LEAD YOU TO THE EXPLORATION OF THE EXOTIC RIVERS OF THE WORLD, THE DISCOVERY OF AN AFRICAN HIDEAWAY, THE TROPICAL MAGIC OF POLYNESIA, OR THE DANGER OF THE STEAMY JUNGLES OF INDIA. AND EVERYWHERE ARE THE SURPRISES OF LUSH FOLIAGE AND THE SOUNDS OF WILD ANIMALS.

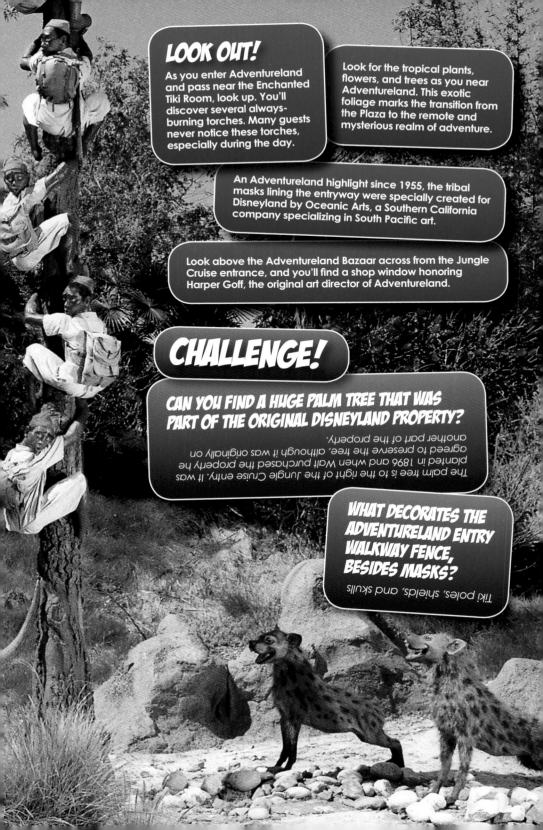

LOOK OUT!

As you enter Adventureland and pass near the Enchanted Tiki Room, look up. You'll discover several always-burning torches. Many guests never notice these torches, especially during the day.

Look for the tropical plants, flowers, and trees as you near Adventureland. This exotic foliage marks the transition from the Plaza to the remote and mysterious realm of adventure.

An Adventureland highlight since 1955, the tribal masks lining the entryway were specially created for Disneyland by Oceanic Arts, a Southern California company specializing in South Pacific art.

Look above the Adventureland Bazaar across from the Jungle Cruise entrance, and you'll find a shop window honoring Harper Goff, the original art director of Adventureland.

CHALLENGE!

CAN YOU FIND A HUGE PALM TREE THAT WAS PART OF THE ORIGINAL DISNEYLAND PROPERTY?

The palm tree is to the right of the Jungle Cruise entry. It was planted in 1896 and when Walt purchased the property he agreed to preserve the tree, although it was originally on another part of the property.

WHAT DECORATES THE ADVENTURELAND ENTRY WALKWAY FENCE, BESIDES MASKS?

Tiki poles, shields, and skulls

WALT DISNEY'S
ENCHANTED TIKI ROOM

WALT DISNEY'S ENCHANTED TIKI ROOM OPENED IN 1963, MARKING THE OFFICIAL DEBUT OF DISNEY'S INNOVATIVE FORM OF THREE-DIMENSIONAL ANIMATION CALLED AUDIO-ANIMATRONICS. THE BIRDS AND FLOWERS CROON IN A CLASSIC MUSICAL SHOW FEATURING SUCH APPROPRIATE NUMBERS AS THE FAMED THEME SONG "THE TIKI, TIKI, TIKI ROOM."

CHECK IT OUT!

The Tiki gods come to life in the tropical paradise known as the Enchanted Tiki Garden outside the building. Listen to the rhyming legends behind such deities as Hina Kuluua, the goddess of rain; Rongo, the god of agriculture; Maui, who roped the playful sun; and Tangaroa, father of all the gods and goddesses.

ASK A CAST MEMBER

When you enter the Tiki Room, ask if you may awaken José the parrot to start the show. (But if you are a boy, don't be offended if José calls you "Senorita"!)

CHALLENGE!

HOW MANY "PERFORMERS" ARE IN THIS ENCHANTING SHOW?

There are 225 animated birds, flowers, plants, and tiki gods.

BESIDES JOSÉ AND THE THREE OTHER HOST PARROTS, WHICH ARE THE OTHER BIRDS THAT HAVE NAMES?

The female cockatoos (Colette, Suzette, Mimi, Gigi, Fifi, and Josephine)

TARZAN'S TREEHOUSE

TARZAN'S TREEHOUSE IS SET IN A VERY "RARE" SPECIES KNOWN AS DISNEYODENDRON SEMPERFLORENS GRANDIS (LATIN FOR "LARGE, EVER-BLOOMING DISNEY TREE"). INSPIRED BY THE 1999 ANIMATED FEATURE TARZAN, THE ATTRACTION FEATURES MOSS AND JUNGLE VINES COVERING THE TREE TO MAKE A FITTING HOME FOR THE "LORD OF THE APES."

CHECK IT OUT!

Watch out for Sabor! But when you find him, get real close and see—and feel—what happens!

In the interactive kitchen, see if you can spot two characters that look as if they might be from *Beauty and the Beast*.

The vintage gramophone is playing the "Swisskapolka," which played in the Swiss Family Treehouse.

As you climb through Tarzan's Treehouse, be sure to ring the bell.

BY THE NUMBERS

Tarzan's Treehouse is 70 feet tall and weighs 150 tons. There are 450 branches with 6,000 hand-applied vinyl leaves.

LOOK OUT!

Watch for the "Mind Thy Head" sign. This is an homage to the original Swiss Family Treehouse, the previous attraction from 1962 to 1999, which had the same warning.

EARS TO YOU

Listen as you pass Baby Tarzan's cradle and notice that the baby's crying includes the famous Tarzan jungle yell.

JUNGLE CRUISE

JUNGLE CRUISE DEBUTED ON THE PARK'S OPENING DAY AND HAS BEEN A FAVORITE WITH "EXPLORERS" EVER SINCE. WALT ORIGINALLY WANTED REAL ANIMALS, BUT ZOOLOGISTS WARNED HIM THAT THE ANIMALS WOULD SLEEP DURING THE DAY, SO HE DECIDED ON LIFELIKE REPLICAS. THE JUNGLE CRUISE RE-CREATES THE SURROUNDINGS OF SUCH EXOTIC RIVERS AS IRRAWADDY, THE RIVER OF BURMA, CAMBODIA'S MEKONG, THE NILE, THE CONGO RIVER IN AFRICA, AND THE RAPIDS OF KILIMANJARO.

THE FACT FILE

The canopy of vegetation over the Jungle Cruise is made up of giant bamboo, ficus, palm, and coral trees. However, when the Jungle Cruise first opened, the plants hadn't had time to grow out. The landscapers planted orange trees upside down—so that their roots would look like gnarled branches.

This classic attraction has seen many updates over the years, including the addition of the Indian Elephant pool in 1962, and an actual re-routing of the river to make room for the Indiana Jones™ Adventure in 1995. Among the most recent additions are the water-churning piranhas.

Every night after the Park's closing, certified divers clean the ears of the hippos!

LOOK OUT!

Keep your eyes on the rafters inside the queue building, and you may see a horn-billed bird and a snake.

The Bo tree (*Ficus religiosa*), a native of India whose history goes back 2,500 years, is a big part of the Cambodian shrine section of the Jungle Cruise. Other vegetation along the attraction includes Gunnera plants, Bod plants, and Black stem trees from New Zealand.

SCAVENGER HUNT

As you approach the Jungle Cruise entrance, find the name of the company that runs the Jungle Cruise, the name of the passenger agent, and the location of the company's home office.

Jungle Navigation Co. Ltd.; J. T. Sharp; 70 Thames Road, London

CHALLENGE!

IN WHAT DECADE IS THE JUNGLE CRUISE SET?

The 1930s

WHAT TYPE OF TIGER DO YOU SEE IN THE ATTRACTION? (DON'T SAY A STRIPED ONE!)

A Bengal tiger

WHAT IS THE JUNGLE CRUISE WATERWAY KNOWN AS?

The "Rivers of the World"

WHAT IS THE WATERFALL IN THE JUNGLE CRUISE CALLED?

Schweitzer Falls

WHO IS IT NAMED AFTER?

Dr. Albert (wait for it) Falls

INDIANA JONES™ ADVENTURE

INSPIRED BY GEORGE LUCAS'S INDIANA JONES™ FILMS, THIS EPIC ADVENTURE IS ONE OF THE LARGEST AND MOST ELABORATE ATTRACTIONS IN DISNEYLAND. THERE ARE MANY JOURNEY COMBINATIONS (TWISTS, TURNS, PLUNGES, SKIDS, FORWARD, BACKWARD, STALLS, ETC.) THAT CAN BE PROGRAMMED INTO THIS THRILLING ADVENTURE, MAKING VIRTUALLY EACH RIDE A UNIQUE EXPERIENCE.

QUEUE VIEWS

As you pass the archaeological office of Professor Jones, who is on the cover of the issue of *Life* magazine?

Mickey Mouse

What is the significance of the crate marked "Deliver to Club Obi Wan"?

It's a sly reference to another famous character created by George Lucas.

What is the significance of the crate marked "990 6753"?

It's the same number that marked the crate holding the Ark of the Covenant in *Raiders of the Lost Ark*.

In the slide show projection room, there's a blue "Eeyore" sign (near the ceiling and partially hidden by bamboo slats). Why?

The attraction was built on the "Eeyore" section of the original parking lot. The Imagineers put in the sign as a tribute.

In the first Skeleton Room of the attraction, there is a skeleton wearing Mickey Mouse ears. To see it, turn to your left and look behind you.

LOOK OUT!

Throughout the attraction are authentic props from the Indiana Jones™ movies. At the entrance is the troop transport that dragged Indy in *Raiders of the Lost Ark*. Other props include an old ore mining car from *Indiana Jones and the Temple of Doom* (near the exit).

THE FACT FILE

The unique written language seen throughout the attraction is called "Maraglyphics."

CHALLENGE!

WHEN YOU BEGIN THE JOURNEY ON YOUR TROOP TRANSIT, THERE ARE THREE POSSIBLE OPTIONS (UNLESS SOMEONE LOOKS INTO THE EYE OF THE GODDESS MARA). WHAT ARE THEY?

The Fountain of Eternal Youth, the Chamber of Earthly Riches, or the Observatory of the Future. (Which one would you choose and why?)

WHEN AND WHERE DOES THE ADVENTURE TAKE PLACE?

1935, in the Temple of the Forbidden Eye on the Lost Delta of India

CHALLENGE YOURSELF!

When you come across a rope near a well, tug on it and listen to what happens!

If you notice holes along the walls of the queue area, look inside!

Touch anything that says not to touch it!

FRONTIERLAND

EVERYONE IS A PIONEER IN FRONTIERLAND, ESPECIALLY AS THEY BLAZE A TRAIL THROUGH THESE ROOTIN' TOOTIN' CHALLENGES. FROM THE WINDSWEPT PEAKS OF BIG THUNDER MOUNTAIN RAILROAD TO THE SHORES OF THE RIVERS OF AMERICA, FRONTIERLAND IS A ROBUST PANORAMA OF SIGHTS AND SOUNDS WAITING TO BE EXPLORED BY WESTERN ADVENTURERS.

THE FACT FILE

Frontierland once had a Marshal's Office honoring Willard P. Bounds, Walt's father-in-law, who had actually been a US Marshal.

The Frontierland gateway is constructed of Ponderosa pine logs.

CHECK IT OUT!

Do you see the elk and deer horns on the roof of the Westward Ho Trading Co.? Elk horns were commonly placed on general stores in the Old West so cowboys coming into town knew immediately where they could buy supplies.

Frontierland boasts the oldest attraction in Disneyland. Look along the banks of the Rivers of America and you'll find a section of a petrified tree. Walt Disney gave this priceless item from the Pike Petrified Forest in Colorado to his wife for their thirty-first wedding anniversary in 1956. How old is the tree? A mere 75 million years.

At the storefront marked "Crockett & Russel Hat Co.," you'll find a window honoring Fess Parker, who played the coonskin cap–wearing pioneer in Walt Disney's Davy Crockett.

CHALLENGE!

CAN YOU FIND FRONTIERLAND'S CANNON?
It's inside the Frontierland gateway, on the right as you enter the gate

WHERE IN FRONTIERLAND CAN YOU FIND A LARGE SIGN FOR LAOD BHANG CO. FIREWORKS FACTORY?
Next to the Stage Door Café

MARK TWAIN RIVERBOAT

THE *MARK TWAIN* RIVERBOAT WAS THE FIRST PADDLE WHEELER BUILT IN THE UNITED STATES IN HALF A CENTURY AND WAS CHRISTENED WITH A BOTTLE OF WATER COLLECTED FROM SEVERAL OF AMERICA'S MAJOR RIVERS.

BY THE NUMBERS

28	height in feet
105	length in feet
150	weight in tons

ASK A CAST MEMBER

Ask one of the attendants if you can help steer the boat or blow the whistle.

SAILING SHIP COLUMBIA

WHEN IT DEBUTED IN DISNEYLAND, THE SAILING SHIP *COLUMBIA* WAS THE FIRST THREE-MASTED WINDJAMMER BUILT IN THE UNITED STATES IN MORE THAN ONE HUNDRED YEARS.

BY THE NUMBERS

84	feet in length of the mainmast
110	feet in length

LOOK OUT!

Belowdecks is a maritime museum re-creating the quarters of an eighteenth-century sailor.

If you see the nighttime spectacular Fantasmic!, watch for the *Columbia* in the "role" of Captain Hook's Pirate Ship.

PIRATE'S LAIR ON TOM SAWYER ISLAND

TOM SAWYER ISLAND OPENED IN 1956. WALT AND TWO CHILDREN PORTRAYING TOM SAWYER AND BECKY THATCHER PLANTED A BOX OF SOIL FROM HANNIBAL, MISSOURI, MOISTENED WITH REAL MISSISSIPPI RIVER WATER ON THE ISLAND IN TRIBUTE TO THE HOME STATE OF TOM SAWYER'S AUTHOR, MARK TWAIN.

WALT WAS HERE

Tom Sawyer Island was designed by Walt Disney himself, with an emphasis on discovery and exploration through footpaths, caves, and bridges.

ASK A CAST MEMBER

Ask any pirate where the marauders have stashed their hoard of loot in Castle Rock.

LOOK OUT!

Quarrelsome pirates Pintel and Ragetti appear as special effects in the form of a spooky head and a skeletal arm. Find them if you dare!

CHECK IT OUT!

Inspired by Tom Sawyer's and Huck Finn's pirate games and their belief that buccaneer treasure was buried on their island, this adventurer's paradise was transformed into Pirate's Lair on Tom Sawyer Island in 2007. Captain Jack Sparrow and his mates from the Pirates of the Caribbean movies have taken over the island.

Explore Dead Man's Grotto and find the ornate chest that holds the heart of Davy Jones. Try and claim it—but beware of the "thump-thump."

Visit Smuggler's Cove and look for sunken treasure alongside a ramshackle barrel bridge. (It can be revealed only by operating a hoist near the sunken ship.)

BIG THUNDER MOUNTAIN RAILROAD

INSPIRED BY THE FANCIFUL RED-ROCK BUTTES OF BRYCE CANYON NATIONAL PARK IN UTAH, BIG THUNDER MOUNTAIN RAILROAD DEBUTED ON SEPTEMBER 2, 1979. TO BUILD THIS TOWERING "NATURAL" FORMATION, IMAGINEERS BECAME EXPERTS ON USING CEMENT AND PAINT TO CREATE REALISTIC-LOOKING ROCKS. BIG THUNDER MOUNTAIN RAILROAD QUICKLY BECAME AN ICONIC LANDMARK OF THE FRONTIERLAND SKYLINE.

WHAT USED TO BE

The Mine Train Thru Nature's Wonderland was in this area of Frontierland from 1960 to 1977. The little town of Rainbow Ridge was held over from that attraction, as were the jumping fish in the pond along Big Thunder Trail.

EARS TO YOU

In the queue area, listen carefully while near the little town of Rainbow Ridge. You may hear conversations between cowboys, barmaids, and miners, and such songs as "Red River Valley."

LOOK OUT!

If a horseshoe symbolizes good luck, what does an upside-down horseshoe mean? Bad luck, of course! See if you can spot the upside-down horseshoe near the beginning of this rip-roarin' attraction . . . and then watch out for trouble ahead.

QUEUE VIEWS

Imagineers scoured swap meets, ghost towns, and abandoned mines to find authentic Gold Rush–era artifacts, including a 1,200-pound cogwheel for breaking down ore, a hand-powered drill press, and a 10-foot-tall 1880 stamp mill.

As you move through the queue, notice the stone walls on either side of you—they were created from one hundred tons of gold ore from the former mining town of Rosamond, California.

CHALLENGE!

WHAT IS THE POPULATION OF BIG THUNDER, THE "BIGGEST LITTLE BOOMTOWN IN THE WEST?"

Thirty-eight

WHAT IS THE NAME OF THE AREA INTO WHICH THE BIG THUNDER MOUNTAIN RAILROAD TRAINS "SPLASH DOWN"?

Dinosaur Gap

NEW ORLEANS SQUARE

WANDER THROUGH NEW ORLEANS SQUARE AND YOU'LL DISCOVER CHALLENGES IN EVERY QUAINT NOOK AND ROMANTIC CRANNY. THE NARROW, WINDING STREETS, INTIMATE COURTYARDS, AND IRON-LACED BALCONIES ARE AUTHENTIC IN EVERY DETAIL. FROM BLOSSOMING MAGNOLIA TREES TO AUTHENTIC GAS LAMPS, THIS PICTURESQUE REALM WILL SURPRISE EVERY EXPLORER WITH THE DELIGHTS OF THE FRENCH QUARTER OF TWO CENTURIES AGO—AND YOU MAY RUN ACROSS A FEW PIRATES AND GHOSTS, TOO.

THE FACT FILE

The Station Master's Office is an exact replica of the one seen in Walt Disney's heartwarming live-action/animated film *So Dear to My Heart* (1949).

CHECK IT OUT!

Look closely over the rooftops of New Orleans Square and you'll spot the masts of a ship.

Balconies in the real French Quarter are renowned for their intricate and artistic iron railings. On the second floor of several of the buildings are props that reveal the inhabitants' occupations: musical instruments, voodoo paraphernalia, and a typewriter.

Check out the ornate initials of Walt and Roy Disney entwined in the wrought-iron design of the balcony above Pirates of the Caribbean.

CAFÉ
ORLÉANS

WALT WAS HERE

Hear that tickety-tick-tap-tap sound coming from the Station Master's Office? That's Walt Disney's Disneyland Opening Day dedication speech being tapped out in landline telegraphy, a predecessor of Morse code.

CHALLENGE!

WHAT ARE THE NAMES OF THE STREETS THAT MAKE UP NEW ORLEANS SQUARE?

Front, Royal, Orleans, and Esplanade

PIRATES OF THE CARIBBEAN

"YE COME SEEKIN' ADVENTURE AND SALTY OLD PIRATES?" PIRATES OF THE CARIBBEAN WAS ORIGINALLY ENVISIONED AS A WALK-THROUGH WITH WAX FIGURES, BUT, AS DEVELOPED BY WALT AND HIS IMAGINEERS, THE ATTRACTION, WHICH OPENED IN 1967, EVOLVED INTO A SWASHBUCKLING SHOWCASE FOR AUDIO-ANIMATRONICS STORYTELLING.

BY THE NUMBERS

It takes three days to empty and refill the "bayou" for repairs and renovations. There are 630,000 gallons of water in the attraction.

There are 53 Audio-Animatronics animals and birds and 75 Audio-Animatronics pirates and villagers (but "We wants the redhead!").

Four hundred thousand gold coins are in the Treasure Cache scene.

CHECK IT OUT!

In 2006, the classic attraction was enhanced with characters from the Pirates of the Caribbean films, which were in turn inspired by the theme park attraction. More than 400 Imagineers worked for three years on the research, planning, and installation of these enhancements. At the same time that the new dialogue of Captain Jack Sparrow, Davy Jones, and Barbossa was recorded by the actors from the films, the original audio tracks were digitally remastered for a crisp and dynamic sound track.

EARS TO YOU

The voice of the talking skull and crossbones before the first waterfall is Imagineer X Atencio, who wrote the attraction's dialogue as well as the lyrics to "Yo Ho (A Pirate's Life for Me)."

Unlike the other characters, the ghostly skeleton pirates in the scenes of the "cursed treasure" do not speak. Dialogue was planned, but it was decided the skeletons made a stronger, spookier statement in silence. When you pass the skeleton crew, you might want to maintain a ghostly silence yourself!

CHALLENGE!

WHAT IS THE NAME OF THE BOARDING AREA?

Laffite's Landing. It refers to Jean Laffite, a pirate captain from 1803 to 1814, who played a key role in the development of New Orleans.

WHAT IS THE NAME OF THE RESTAURANT INSIDE THE ATTRACTION?

The Blue Bayou

OTHER THAN JACK SPARROW AND BARBOSSA, WHAT OTHER CHARACTERS IN THE ATTRACTION HAVE NAMES?

Davy Jones, Carlos the Mayor, and Old Bill (with the cats)

THE HAUNTED MANSION

"WELCOME, FOOLISH MORTALS!" THE HAUNTED MANSION WAS IN THE PLANNING STAGES FOR MANY YEARS BEFORE THE ATTRACTION ACTUALLY OPENED. AT FIRST, THE IMAGINEERS ENVISIONED A TRADITIONAL, RUN-DOWN HAUNTED HOUSE, BUT WALT WANTED IT TO BE AS NEAT AND CLEAN AS THE REST OF DISNEYLAND. "WE'LL TAKE CARE OF THE OUTSIDE," HE SAID, "AND LET THE GHOSTS TAKE CARE OF THE INSIDE." THE HAUNTED MANSION OPENED TO THE PUBLIC IN 1969 AND HAS BEEN A SPOOK-TACULAR SUCCESS EVER SINCE.

QUEUE VIEWS

Check out the tombstones as you make your way toward the entrance. There are two sections to the graveyard: a pet cemetery and crypts against the wall. There are many more tombstones inside!

EARS TO YOU

The seer in the crystal ball, Madame Leota, has the face of the aptly named Imagineer Leota Toombs, who also appears as (and gives voice to) "Little Leota" at the end of the attraction. ("Hurry back. . . . Be sure to bring your death certificate.") The voice of Madame Leota is Eleanor Audley, who voiced Cinderella's wicked Stepmother and Maleficent in *Sleeping Beauty*.

CHECK IT OUT!

In 2006, a new Attic sequence was added to the attraction, telling the ghostly tale of Constance, also known as the "Black Widow" Bride. Watch (or watch out!) for this "constant" bride, and the portraits of her former husbands, who lost their heads over her!

LOOK OUT!

Not only is the ghostly clock in the long hallway always striking "13" but if you look closely, you'll see that its face is being eaten by a demon whose tail is the pendulum.

The ghostly organ in the ballroom was originally used in Walt Disney's *20,000 Leagues Under the Sea* (1954).

CHALLENGE!

WHAT ARE THE HAUNTED MANSION RIDE VEHICLES CALLED?

Doom Buggies

HOW MANY GHOSTS "LIVE" IN THE HAUNTED MANSION?

999 ("But there is always room for a thousand...")

HOW MANY TIMES DO YOU SEE THE RAVEN THROUGHOUT THE ATTRACTION? HINT: THE RAVEN USUALLY APPEARS WHENEVER THE GHOST HOST SPEAKS.

Four

CRITTER COUNTRY

YOU'LL FIND CRITTER COUNTRY NESTLED IN A LAZY CORNER OF THE BACKWOODS. THIS COZY AREA OF SHADY TREES AND COOL STREAMS IS THE PERFECT SETTING FOR ENJOYING LONG LAZY AFTERNOONS— BUT THERE ARE PLENTY OF CHALLENGES TO KEEP YOU ON YOUR TOES AS YOU MEET ALLIGATORS, OWLS, FROGS, AND A WHOLE FOREST FULL OF FRIENDLY CRITTERS. YOU CAN SPLASH DOWN WITH WILY BRER RABBIT, AND EVEN EXPLORE THE HUNDRED ACRE WOOD AND GET A BEAR HUG FROM LOVABLE WINNIE THE POOH. YOU'LL DISCOVER TEASERS AND TREATS THROUGHOUT THIS NEIGHBORLY NECK OF THE WOODS.

LOOK OUT!

As you visit Critter Country, keep your eyes peeled for the small-scale critter houses along the running brook.

CRITTER COUNTRY

CHALLENGE!

CAN YOU NAME THE ANIMALS DEPICTED IN THE RUSTIC CRITTER COUNTRY MARQUEE SIGN?

Fox, bear, turtle, squirrel, rabbit, mouse

SPLASH MOUNTAIN

INSPIRED BY THE ANIMATED ANTICS OF BRER RABBIT IN WALT DISNEY'S *SONG OF THE SOUTH*, SPLASH MOUNTAIN IS ONE OF THE WORLD'S TALLEST AND SHARPEST FLUME DROPS. TRAVELERS RIDE IN A HOLLOWED-OUT LOG, ONLY TO PLUMMET FROM THE LAUGHIN' PLACE TO THE BRIAR PATCH AND ON TO A BACKWOODS BAYOU BASH.

LOOK OUT!

There's a sign to the right side of the logs as you splash down that reads "Drop in Again Sometime."

QUEUE VIEWS

Notice that hanging on the walls of the queue are thoughts and sayings from the great storyteller Uncle Remus. In *Song of the South* Uncle Remus was portrayed by James Baskett, who was given an honorary Oscar for his performance.

EARS TO YOU

When Splash Mountain was being created, the original voice of Brer Bear from *Song of the South*, Nick Stewart, returned to give voice to the character, more than five decades after having originally created the vocal role.

Before the first drop at Slippin' Falls, you'll see a cave. Listen carefully and you'll hear Brer Bear snoring. That snore is a tribute to the original entrance to Bear Country (as Critter Country was called from 1972 through 1988), where a bear named Rufus could be heard snoring from within a cave. (The snoring was recorded in the 1930s for *Snow White and the Seven Dwarfs* but was never used in that film.)

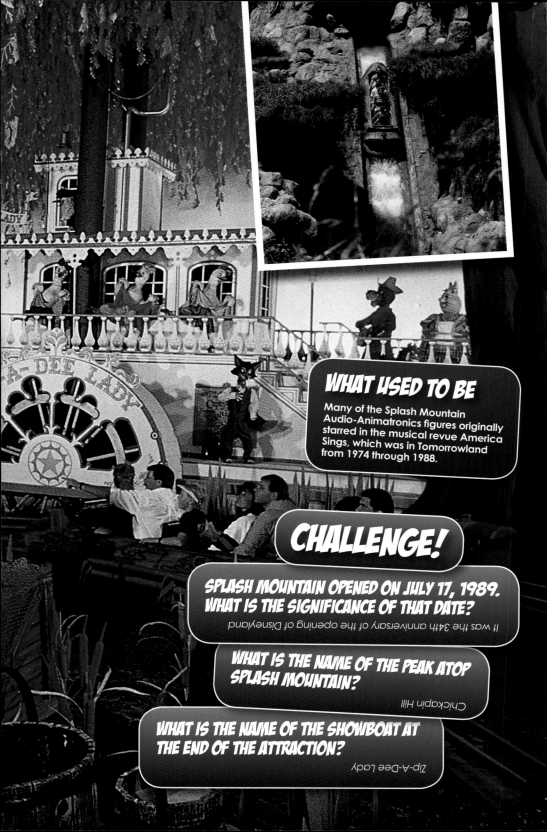

WHAT USED TO BE

Many of the Splash Mountain Audio-Animatronics figures originally starred in the musical revue America Sings, which was in Tomorrowland from 1974 through 1988.

CHALLENGE!

SPLASH MOUNTAIN OPENED ON JULY 17, 1989. WHAT IS THE SIGNIFICANCE OF THAT DATE?

It was the 34th anniversary of the opening of Disneyland

WHAT IS THE NAME OF THE PEAK ATOP SPLASH MOUNTAIN?

Chickapin Hill

WHAT IS THE NAME OF THE SHOWBOAT AT THE END OF THE ATTRACTION?

Zip-A-Dee Lady

THE MANY ADVENTURES OF WINNIE THE POOH

THIS WHIMSICAL ATTRACTION FEATURES POOH AND HIS ENDEARING FRIENDS IN A COLORFUL JOURNEY THROUGH A BLUSTERY DAY, A FLOODY NIGHT, AND A NIGHTMARE FULL OF HEFFALUMPS AND WOOZLES—ALL IN A QUEST FOR THAT GOLDEN TREASURE, "HUNNY."

EARS TO YOU

As you wait to board the ride vehicles, called "beehicles," you'll hear the faint buzzing of bees.

LOOK OUT!

Can you spot three very special "guests?" The trophy heads of Buff the buffalo, Max the elk, and Melvin the moose from the Country Bear Jamboree, the attraction's former tenants, are hanging around—but you really have to look for them!

CHALLENGE!

WHAT DOES THE SIGN OVER POOH'S HOUSE SAY?

"Mr. Sanders." It's the name Pooh lives under.

WHAT DOES THE SIGN OUTSIDE PIGLET'S HOUSE SAY?

"Trespassers Will." (For his grandfather "Trespassers William.")

DAVY CROCKETT'S EXPLORER CANOES

DAVY CROCKETT BECAME A DISNEY HERO IN THE FAMOUS AND ENORMOUSLY POPULAR TV PROGRAMS WALT DISNEY PRODUCED FROM 1954 THROUGH 1956. THE ATTRACTION FIRST OPENED ON JULY 4, 1956, AS INDIAN WAR CANOES. THE NAME WAS CHANGED TO DAVY CROCKETT'S EXPLORER CANOES AND RE-OPENED ON MAY 19, 1971. THERE ARE NINE 35-FOOT FIBERGLASS CANOES THAT EMBARK ON A 2,400-FOOT TRIP ALONG THE RIVERS OF AMERICA.

THE FACT FILE

Davy Crockett Explorer Canoes is one of only two attractions to have been in three different lands, without ever having moved from the same basic location! Through the years, the canoes have been considered part of Frontierland, Bear Country, and Critter Country.

CHECK IT OUT!

The Davy Crockett Explorer Canoes are one of the most hands-on attractions in all of Disneyland. The canoes are not complete without explorers—that's you! The bowman will teach you to use the oars to power the canoes.

CHALLENGE!

WHAT ARE THE OARSMEN CALLED?

The helmsman or bowman and the stem man. (For their actual names, look at their name tags!)

CHALLENGE YOURSELF!

If you're in Disneyland on a day when the Explorer Canoes are operating, set yourself a special goal: ride all the transportation on the Rivers of America! Depending on the season, this could include the *Mark Twain* riverboat, the Sailing Ship *Columbia*, and the Tom Sawyer Rafts, as well as the canoes. After your special voyages, you can call yourself an authentic river pioneer!

FANTASYLAND

FANTASYLAND OVERFLOWS WITH DELIGHTFUL DETAILS
WAITING TO BE DISCOVERED WITHIN THE MAGICAL,
OLD-WORLD SETTING OF THE "HAPPIEST KINGDOM OF
THEM ALL." YOU'LL BE CHALLENGED BY TIDBITS AND
TREASURES FOUND THROUGHOUT THIS FANCIFUL REALM
OF FANTASTIC STORIES AND FABULOUS LORE.
FLY TO NEVER LAND, TAKE A SPIN IN A GIANT TEACUP, OR
BRAVE THE ICY THRILLS OF THE MATTERHORN BOBSLEDS,
AS YOU SEEK OUT THE HIDDEN WONDERS OF THIS
LAND OF DREAMS COME TRUE.

CHALLENGE YOURSELF!

Stand in the outer courtyard (in front of the moat) and walk
around the giant compass inlaid on the walkway. Read the
words out loud and when you are done, stand in the center
and make a wish on the "star."

Want to go on a "timely" treasure hunt? Look
for the plaque that marks the spot where the
Disneyland Time Capsule is buried.

The plaque is in the Sleeping Beauty Castle
Courtyard. Sealed on the 40th anniversary of
Disneyland, and containing all kinds of Disneyland
goodies including pins, buttons, and photos, this
special time capsule is scheduled to be opened
40 years from the day it was sealed.

Can you figure out when that will be? If the
Park opened in 1955 . . . ?

2035

THE FACT FILE

Though the "Fantasy in the Sky" fireworks spectacular was introduced in 1956, Tinker Bell's first flight as part of the show was in 1961. The first Tinker Bell was Tiny Kline, a 70-year-old former circus aerialist.

SLEEPING BEAUTY CASTLE

INSPIRED IN PART BY ACTUAL MEDIEVAL EUROPEAN CASTLES, SUCH AS NEUSCHWANSTEIN CASTLE IN BAVARIA, SLEEPING BEAUTY CASTLE WAS DELIBERATELY DESIGNED SMALLER IN SCALE AS WALT WANTED IT TO FEEL FRIENDLY AND WELCOMING. THE DRAWBRIDGE OF THE CASTLE WAS RAISED, THEN LOWERED FOR ONLY THE SECOND TIME AS PART OF THE REDEDICATION CEREMONIES FOR FANTASYLAND IN 1983. THE FIRST TIME WAS ON OPENING DAY, JULY 17, 1955.

WALT WAS HERE

The Disney family crest is over the castle entrance archway. What do you think the three lions represent? That's right, courage!

LOOK OUT!

The castle seems taller than its 77-foot height because its "stones" are larger at the foundation and smaller on the turrets, another example of forced perspective.

Look for the swans swimming in the moat. The plants lining the moat are junipers, which are one of the few plants swans won't eat!

The squirrel-shaped golden waterspouts on the front of the castle were inspired by Aurora's (Sleeping Beauty's) woodland friends.

CHALLENGE!

CAN YOU NAME ALL THREE OF THE GOOD FAIRIES?

Flora, Fauna, and Merryweather

HOW MANY STONES WERE USED TO BUILD THE CASTLE?

None! The outside stonework is actually made out of cement, plaster, and fiberglass

KING ARTHUR CARROUSEL

ONE OF THE LARGEST CARROUSELS IN THE WORLD, KING ARTHUR CARROUSEL CAME FROM CANADA. THE ORIGINAL TURNTABLE WAS MADE AROUND 1875 BY THE DENTZEL COMPANY. MOST OF THE HAND-CARVED, HAND-PAINTED HORSES WERE CREATED IN GERMANY AND ARE BETWEEN 90 AND 110 YEARS OLD.

THE FACT FILE

Each of the horses has a name— a complete list is available at City Hall. The lead horse's name is Jingles. A carrousel's lead horse is always the most ornate, and using a string of bells to delineate it is very traditional.

CHALLENGE!

WHAT'S THE DIFFERENCE BETWEEN A MERRY-GO-ROUND AND A CARROUSEL?

A merry-go-round has different types of animals and turns clockwise, while a carrousel features only horses and spins counterclockwise.

THE SWORD IN THE STONE CEREMONY IS HELD DAILY AS MERLIN THE MAGICIAN PICKS A GIRL OR BOY TO PROVE HIM- OR HERSELF MONARCH OF THE LAND BY TRYING TO PULL THE ENCHANTED SWORD FROM THE STONE.

THE SWORD IN THE STONE

CHALLENGE!

WHAT WAS THE NICKNAME OF KING ARTHUR WHEN HE WAS A BOY?

Wart

SNOW WHITE'S SCARY ADVENTURES

THIS JOURNEY INTO THE STORY OF WALT DISNEY'S FIRST ANIMATED FEATURE WAS ORIGINALLY ENTITLED SNOW WHITE'S ADVENTURES. SOME GUESTS FOUND THE WICKED DEEDS OF THE EVIL QUEEN QUITE FRIGHTENING SO A WARNING SIGN WAS ADDED. IN 1983, THE NAME WAS CHANGED TO SNOW WHITE'S SCARY ADVENTURES, JUST TO BE SURE.

THE FACT FILE

Snow White herself did not appear in her own attraction until 1983. Why? Because the original idea was that each guest was taking the place of Snow White and experiencing the lovely princess's adventures.

LOOK OUT!

Watch the window with the red curtains in the second story of the attraction's exterior. Every so often you'll see the Evil Queen glare out the window. The next time she looks out, stare back at her and see if anyone joins you.

CHALLENGE YOURSELF!

As you wait to enter the attraction, touch the golden apple above the open spell book at the entrance and hear what happens!

CHALLENGE!

CAN YOU NAME ALL SEVEN DWARFS?

Happy, Grumpy, Sleepy, Sneezy, Bashful, Doc, and Dopey

WHICH DWARF DOESN'T SPEAK?

Dopey

PINOCCHIO'S DARING JOURNEY

THIS FANCIFUL ADVENTURE WAS ADDED IN 1983 AS PART OF THE NEW FANTASYLAND. BEFORE THE RENOVATION, FANTASYLAND WAS THEMED AS A LIVELY MEDIEVAL FAIR, WITH TENTS, BANNERS, AND FLAGS. BUT IT DIDN'T HAVE THE RICH LOOK OF A WORLD OF STORYBOOK FANTASY THAT WALT HAD ORIGINALLY ENVISIONED, SO FANTASYLAND WAS REDESIGNED TO REFLECT THE STYLE AND SETTINGS.

LOOK OUT!

Look carefully on the attraction's roof for a weathervane in the shape of Monstro the Whale.

CHALLENGE!

NOTICE THE MARIONETTE SHOW OVER THE ENTRANCE TO PINOCCHIO'S DARING JOURNEY. WHAT WAS THE NAME OF THE EVIL PUPPETEER WHO RAN THE MARIONETTE SHOW? (ANYONE WHO SAYS GEPPETTO IS IMMEDIATELY DISQUALIFIED!)

Stromboli

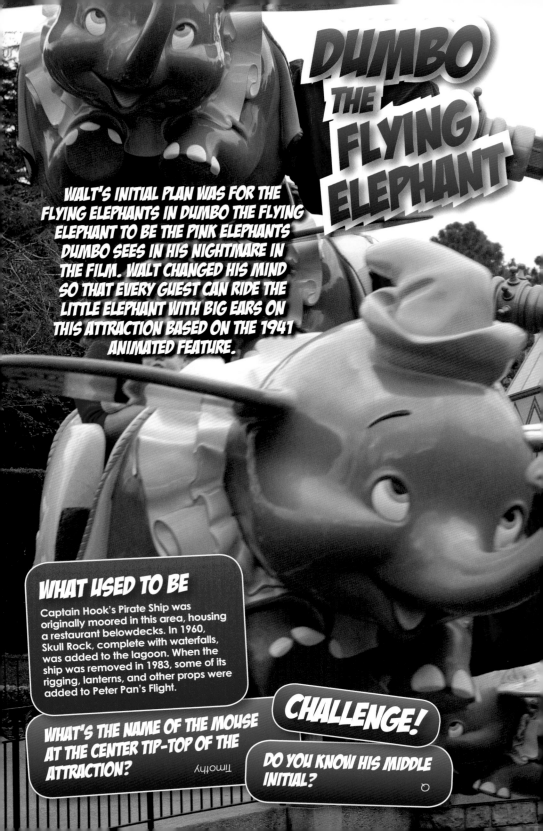

DUMBO THE FLYING ELEPHANT

WALT'S INITIAL PLAN WAS FOR THE FLYING ELEPHANTS IN DUMBO THE FLYING ELEPHANT TO BE THE PINK ELEPHANTS DUMBO SEES IN HIS NIGHTMARE IN THE FILM. WALT CHANGED HIS MIND SO THAT EVERY GUEST CAN RIDE THE LITTLE ELEPHANT WITH BIG EARS ON THIS ATTRACTION BASED ON THE 1941 ANIMATED FEATURE.

WHAT USED TO BE

Captain Hook's Pirate Ship was originally moored in this area, housing a restaurant belowdecks. In 1960, Skull Rock, complete with waterfalls, was added to the lagoon. When the ship was removed in 1983, some of its rigging, lanterns, and other props were added to Peter Pan's Flight.

WHAT'S THE NAME OF THE MOUSE AT THE CENTER TIP-TOP OF THE ATTRACTION?

Timothy

CHALLENGE!

DO YOU KNOW HIS MIDDLE INITIAL?

Q

CASEY JR. CIRCUS TRAIN

CASEY JR. WAS ORIGINALLY MEANT TO BE THE FIRST ROLLER COASTER IN DISNEYLAND PARK. TEST RUNS WERE CONDUCTED, BUT TECHNICAL PROBLEMS PUT A STOP TO THOSE INITIAL PLANS. THE CASEY JR. CIRCUS TRAIN FIRST STARTED CHUG-CHUGGING ON JULY 31, 1955.

THE FACT FILE

The train's ornate sleigh benches came from the original merry-go-round that was used to create King Arthur Carrousel.

STORYBOOK LAND CANAL BOATS

A UNIQUE VOYAGE PAST MINIATURE SCENES FROM DISNEY ANIMATED CLASSICS, THIS CHARMING ATTRACTION, INSPIRED BY WALT DISNEY'S HOBBY OF COLLECTING MINIATURES AND BUILDING SMALL-SCALE MODELS AND SETS, OPENED IN 1956.

LOOK OUT!

Check out the tiny toys in Geppetto's Workshop window and the goods in the peddler's kiosk in the city of Agrabah.

As you float past the Alice in Wonderland section of Storybook Land, look for the White Rabbit's tiny mailbox.

Can you spot the tallest Storybook Land structure? It's Cinderella Castle.

"IT'S A SMALL WORLD"

BY THE NUMBERS

Fifty gardeners create the shrub topiaries, which take from 3 to 5 years each. There are four individual shrubs in the topiary elephant, with the longest shrub being the ears and trunk.

There are 100 regions of the world represented in the attraction, and more than 300 Audio-Animatronics doll-like figures.

LOOK OUT!

Every quarter hour, the whimsical clock outside strikes, with music and sound effects, and a parade of international toylike figures march out. It was Walt Disney's idea to have 24 figures— one for each hour of the day.

One of Walt's favorite artists, Mary Blair, worked extensively on "it's a small world." There's a tribute to her within the attraction—the small blond doll wearing black boots and a poncho halfway up the Eiffel Tower.

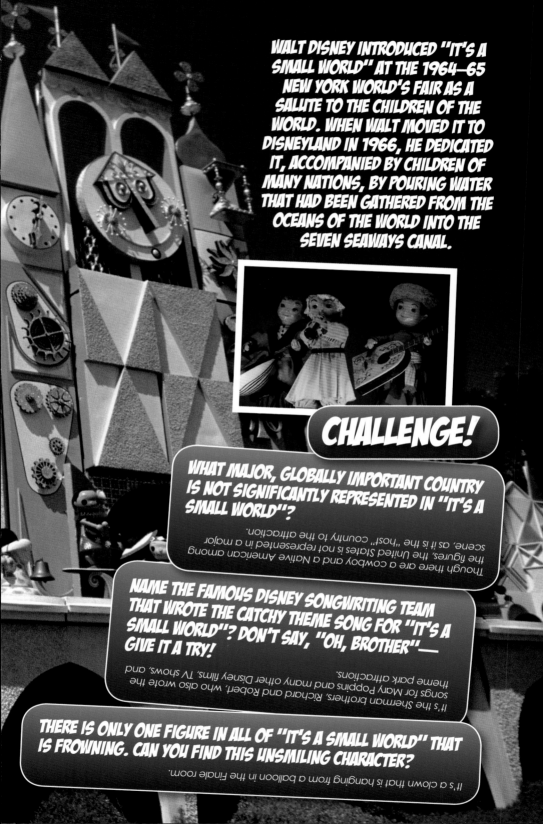

WALT DISNEY INTRODUCED "IT'S A SMALL WORLD" AT THE 1964—65 NEW YORK WORLD'S FAIR AS A SALUTE TO THE CHILDREN OF THE WORLD. WHEN WALT MOVED IT TO DISNEYLAND IN 1966, HE DEDICATED IT, ACCOMPANIED BY CHILDREN OF MANY NATIONS, BY POURING WATER THAT HAD BEEN GATHERED FROM THE OCEANS OF THE WORLD INTO THE SEVEN SEAWAYS CANAL.

CHALLENGE!

WHAT MAJOR, GLOBALLY IMPORTANT COUNTRY IS NOT SIGNIFICANTLY REPRESENTED IN "IT'S A SMALL WORLD"?

Though there are a cowboy and a Native American among the figures, the United States is not represented in a major scene, as it is the "host" country to the attraction.

NAME THE FAMOUS DISNEY SONGWRITING TEAM THAT WROTE THE CATCHY THEME SONG FOR "IT'S A SMALL WORLD"? DON'T SAY, "OH, BROTHER"___ GIVE IT A TRY!

It's the Sherman brothers, Richard and Robert, who also wrote the songs for Mary Poppins and many other Disney films, TV shows, and theme park attractions.

THERE IS ONLY ONE FIGURE IN ALL OF "IT'S A SMALL WORLD" THAT IS FROWNING. CAN YOU FIND THIS UNSMILING CHARACTER?

It's a clown that is hanging from a balloon in the finale room.

MATTERHORN BOBSLEDS

THOUGH IT TOWERS OVER THE MAGIC KINGDOM, MATTERHORN MOUNTAIN IS 100 TIMES SMALLER THAN THE REAL ONE. THIS THRILLING "BOBSLED RIDE" ATTRACTION WAS INSPIRED BY THE FILM *THIRD MAN ON THE MOUNTAIN* (1959). THE MATTERHORN BOBSLEDS ATTRACTION WAS DEDICATED ON JUNE 14, 1959, AND WAS THE FIRST THRILL RIDE IN DISNEYLAND.

CHECK IT OUT!

Occasionally, mountain climbers (including Mickey and Goofy) ascend the peak, wearing native Swiss costumes and using authentic mountain climbers' gear.

THE FACT FILE

Matterhorn Bobsleds uses forced perspective to trick the eye into perceiving it as being larger than it actually is. The Colorado spruce trees and piñon pines at the Matterhorn's "timberline" are much smaller than the ones below.

The Abominable Snowman was added in 1978, along with the ice cavern and glowing ice crystals. The slogan used in commercials, signs, and billboards to promote the addition of the Snowman was "What's Gotten into the Matterhorn?"

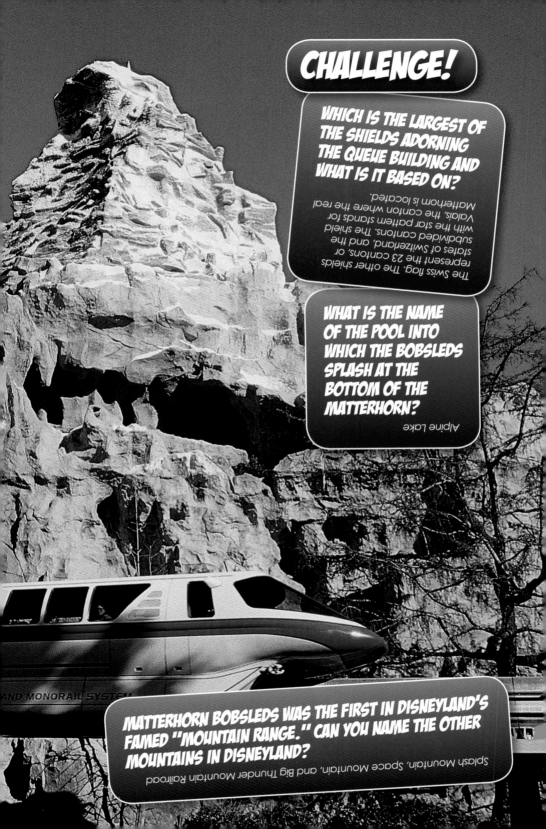

ALICE IN WONDERLAND

THE ALICE IN WONDERLAND ATTRACTION WAS INSPIRED BY WALT DISNEY'S 1951 ANIMATED CLASSIC. THIS ZANY JOURNEY THROUGH THE NONSENSICAL WORLD OF WONDERLAND OPENED IN 1958, THREE YEARS AFTER THE REST OF FANTASYLAND. IN KEEPING WITH THE TRADITION OF LATENESS THAT'S ASSOCIATED WITH THE WHITE RABBIT CHARACTER, A NEWLY REDESIGNED ATTRACTION OPENED IN 1984—A YEAR AFTER THE REST OF THE "NEW" FANTASYLAND WAS UNVEILED IN 1983.

THE FACT FILE

Alice in Wonderland is one of the few Disney theme park attractions unique to Disneyland.

EARS TO YOU

The original voice of Alice from Walt Disney's animated feature Alice in Wonderland, Kathryn Beaumont, returned three decades later to re-create the vocal role for the new version of the Disneyland attraction.

LOOK OUT!

Hunt for the rabbit tracks that are found throughout the attraction.

CHALLENGE YOURSELF!

As you wait in line, wish everyone around you a merry unbirthday!

MAD TEA PARTY

LOOK OUT!
The plants outside the Mad Tea Party spell ALICE.

The crooked smokestacks look like rabbit ears.

Watch the mirror inside the Mad Hatter Hat Shop. When you see the Cheshire Cat grinning at you "through the looking glass," be sure to grin back at him!

ONE OF THE SIGNATURE FANTASYLAND ATTRACTIONS, THE MAD TEA PARTY IS ALSO ONE OF THE ORIGINAL TWENTY OPENING DAY ATTRACTIONS. IN THIS WACKY RIDE, INSPIRED BY THE TEA PARTY SEQUENCE FROM ALICE IN WONDERLAND, GUESTS CAN SPIN CRAZILY IN THEIR GIANT TEACUPS.

SNOW WHITE GROTTO

THE WHITE MARBLE SCULPTURES OF THE PRINCESS AND HER FRIENDS WERE CARVED IN ITALY AND PRESENTED TO WALT DISNEY, BUT, UNFORTUNATELY, THE DWARFS WERE AS LARGE AS SNOW WHITE. THE IMAGINEERS SOLVED THAT PROBLEM BY CAREFUL DESIGN OF THE GROTTO AND PLACEMENT OF THE SNOW WHITE STATUE ON TOP.

LOOK OUT!

Watch the pool in the grotto carefully. Every so often, some fanciful fish spin up out of the pool, spouting water from their mouths.

CHECK IT OUT!

At the Wishing Well, you can hear Snow White singing "I'm Wishing." It's actually the original voice of the character, Adriana Caselotti.

PETER PAN'S FLIGHT

BASED ON WALT DISNEY'S 1953 ANIMATED CLASSIC, THIS FANCIFUL ATTRACTION ALLOWS GUESTS TO BOARD A PIRATE GALLEON AND FLY OVER LONDON FOR AN ENCHANTING VISIT TO NEVER LAND.

CHALLENGE!

WHAT DO THE ALPHABET BLOCKS SPELL IN THE NURSERY SCENE AT THE BEGINNING OF THE RIDE? YOU'LL NEED TO READ THEM BACKWARD!

DISNEY

WHAT ARE THE DIRECTIONS TO NEVER LAND?

Second star to the right and straight on till morning

MR. TOAD'S WILD RIDE

GUESTS TAKE A MADCAP TRIP THROUGH TOAD HALL AND THE ENGLISH COUNTRYSIDE IN THIS JAUNTY JOURNEY.

CHALLENGE!

WHAT IS THE FULL NAME OF MR. TOAD'S HORSE?

Cyril Proudbottom

LOOK OUT!

Sherlock Holmes appears as a shadow in a second-story window.

WHAT IS MR. TOAD'S FULL NAME?

J. Thaddeus Toad, Esq.

WHERE AND WHAT IS THE INSIGNIA OF MR. TOAD'S COAT OF ARMS?

Over the entryway, it says, "Toadi Acceleratio Semper Absurda." That's Latin for "Speeding with Toad is always absurd."

MICKEY'S TOONTOWN

YOU'LL FEEL A BIT "GOOFY" AS YOU EXPLORE THE KOOKY NOOKS AND OFF-KILTER CRANNIES OF THIS CARTOONY COMMUNITY. LEGEND HAS IT THAT MICKEY MOUSE FOUNDED TOONTOWN AS A RETREAT FROM THE LIGHTS OF HOLLYWOOD. UNTIL ITS OPENING IN 1993, TOONTOWN WAS KEPT A SECRET FROM EVERY HUMAN EXCEPT WALT DISNEY. FORTUNATELY, AS DISNEYLAND PARK GREW, MICKEY DECIDED TO OPEN TOONTOWN TO EVERYONE. HERE, YOUR FAVORITE ANIMATED STARS LIVE, WORK, AND PLAY—AND EVERY ZANY DETAIL WILL TICKLE YOUR FUNNY BONE.

THE FACT FILE

Mickey's Toontown is divided into three areas: Downtown to the east, Mickey's Neighborhood in the west, and Toon Square in the middle.

SCAVENGER HUNT

Find the Laugh-O-Meter in front of the Gag Factory and check out the pillars at the back of the shop.

Find the Police Phone near the Power Company to hear a police dispatch. Warning: try to open the Power Company door at your own risk!

Step on the "mouse-hole" cover near the Post Office and listen carefully.

WALT WAS HERE

To see Walt's window in Toontown, look for the glass pane in the library window that reads Laugh-O-gram Films Inc. Laugh-O-gram Films was Walt's first animation studio in Kansas City, Missouri.

TOWN

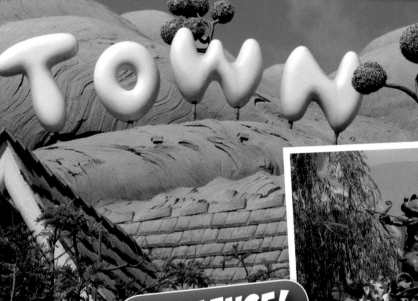

CHALLENGE!

WHAT IS THE CLOCK ABOVE CITY HALL CALLED?

The Clockenspiel. It rings bells and blows whistles to announce when a Disney character is coming out of City Hall to meet-and-greet.

WHAT WAS THE ONE RULE THE DISNEY IMAGINEERS FOLLOWED IN DESIGNING THE BUILDINGS IN MICKEY'S TOONTOWN?

No rulers! No straight lines are used on the buildings, to make them as "cartoony," as possible.

WHAT DOES THE SIGN OVER THE ENTRANCE TO MICKEY'S TOONTOWN THAT READS "DAR" STAND FOR?

Daughters of the Animated Reel

NAME THREE OTHER SIGNS AT THE ENTRANCE.

Loyal Knights of the Inkwell, Optimist Intoontional, and the Benevolent and Protective Order of the Mouse

MICKEY'S HOUSE AND MOVIE BARN

WELCOME TO MICKEY'S HOUSE! THIS HAPPY HOME IS A FUN PLACE TO VISIT. THEN CONTINUE TO MICKEY'S MOVIE BARN AND MEET THE "BIG CHEESE" HIMSELF!

LOOK OUT!

In Mickey's garden, the carrots disappear. (You may even spot who's responsible!)

QUEUE VIEWS

On the way to meeting Mickey, how many of his movie props can you identify?

Some of the props include the plane from Mickey's first short film, Plane Crazy, costumes from The Band Concert, the bucket-carrying brooms from Fantasia, a lamppost, a cuckoo clock, and the Magic Mirror where Mickey Mouse himself appears!

CHALLENGE!

WHAT IS THE EXACT ADDRESS OF MICKEY MOUSE'S HOUSE?

1 Neighborhood Lane (Check out the letters on the table inside.)

WHAT IS THE LICENSE PLATE ON MICKEY'S CAR?

MICKEY1

WHERE IN MICKEY'S MOVIE BARN DO YOU HEAR DONALD AND GOOFY?

In the screening room

MINNIE'S HOUSE

EVERYONE'S SWEETHEART LIVES IN A HOUSE AS SWEET AND CHARMING AS MISS MINNIE HERSELF—AND YOU'RE INVITED TO DROP BY FOR A VISIT.

CHALLENGE!

WHAT ARE THE NAMES OF THE CHEESES IN MINNIE'S FRIDGE?

Jack, Bob, Mouserella, True Bleu, Gouda, Not So Gouda, and The Big Cheese

EARS TO YOU

As you pass Minnie's wishing well, be prepared with a snappy comeback, as the well sometimes speaks!

Be sure to listen to the messages on Minnie's answering machine.

CHALLENGE YOURSELF!

While visiting Minnie's sweetheart of a house, take a minute or two and design some fashions on her dressing-room computer.

In the kitchen, make her cake rise in the oven and start the wash cycle in the dishwasher.

DONALD'S BOAT

WADDLE ABOARD DONALD'S BOAT, THE SLIGHTLY SEAWORTHY, MISS DAISY, FOR SOME SHIPSHAPE FUN.

CHALLENGE YOUR KIDS!

Steer the ship's wheel and watch the compass.

EARS TO YOU

Listen for Donald's voice to quack you up as it squawks out of the speaker in the pilothouse. You may even hear Donald having a conversation with his nephews.

CHALLENGE!

BESIDES DONALD, WHO IS IN THE FRAMED PHOTOS ON THE WALL NEAR DONALD'S HAMMOCK?

Donald's nephews — Huey, Dewey, and Louie — Daisy, and Walt Disney

WHERE DOES DONALD DUCK LIVE?

Nearby, in Duckburg

WHAT IS UNIQUE ABOUT THE "PORTRAIT" OF DONALD THAT IS ON A BUOY OUTSIDE HIS BOAT?

It's a life preserver

WHAT IS HUNG ON THE RIGGING OF THE MISS DAISY BESIDES FLAGS?

Donald's shirt and hat, and lanterns

GOOFY'S PLAYHOUSE

SCAVENGER HUNT

Tour the Goofy goings-on inside. See if you can spot the following: a Christmas tree, a kite, an open umbrella, a baseball mitt with a ball-sized hole in it, a musket with a cork hanging out of it, a framed picture of Goofy with a surfboard. What other goofy details can you find?

VISIT THE GOOFIEST HOUSE IN THE NEIGHBORHOOD, AND YOU'LL FIND YOURSELF SAYING, "GAWRSH!"

As you look at the funny-faced jack-o'-lanterns in Goofy's pumpkin patch, can you pick out the pumpkin that is wearing glasses? This is a pumpkin designed to look like Jack Lindquist, the first president of Disneyland.

LOOK OUT!

Take a goofy gander at the safety sign reading, "Supervise Children at all times." Do you notice anything special about the symbol for the child?

The child is wearing Mickey Mouse ears.

CHALLENGE!

WHAT IS IN THE TEETH OF THE FRAMED FISH INSIDE GOOFY'S PLAYHOUSE?

A pair of polka-dotted shorts

WHAT IS THE TITLE OF THE SHEET MUSIC ON THE PIANO INSIDE GOOFY'S PLAYHOUSE?

Silly Scales in G

ROGER RABBIT'S CARTOON SPIN

THIS WACKY JAUNT THROUGH THE WORLD OF THE 1988 FILM *WHO FRAMED ROGER RABBIT?* WAS THE FIRST NEW DARK RIDE INTRODUCED IN DISNEYLAND IN THE DECADE IT DEBUTED, IN 1994. THE CABS CAN SPIN 360 DEGREES, SO THE IMAGINEERS CREATED A P-P-P-PLETHORA OF DETAILS TO BE SEEN IN EVERY DIRECTION DURING THIS WHIRLING, TWIRLING ADVENTURE. WATCH OUT FOR THE DIP!

CHALLENGE!

QUEUE VIEWS

How many Disney characters, places, or terms can you identify by the license plates in the queue area's garage? For example, 101 DLMN is *One Hundred and One Dalmatians*.

2N Town	(Toontown)
I M L8	(I'm late – the White Rabbit!)
Mr. Toad	(of the Wild Ride!)
CAP 10 HK	(Captain Hook)
3 LIL PIGS	(Three Little Pigs)
BB Wolf	(Big Bad Wolf)
1DRLAND	(Wonderland)
L MERM8	(Little Mermaid)
FAN T C	(Fantasy)
RS2CAT	(Aristocats)
ZPD2DA	("Zip-A-Dee-Doo-Dah")
1D N PTR	(Wendy and Peter Pan)

WHO DO YOU RIDE ALONG WITH ON ROGER RABBIT'S CARTOON SPIN?

Lenny the Cab

WHO IS LENNY'S COUSIN?

Benny the Cab, from the film, *Who Framed Roger Rabbit!*

WHAT STORE DO YOU CRASH THROUGH?

The Bulldog China Shop

CHIP N' DALE'S TREEHOUSE

KIDS WILL GO NUTTY ABOUT THIS PLAY PLACE WHERE A SPIRAL STAIRCASE TAKES THEM TO A GREAT VIEW OF THE PARK.

CHECK IT OUT!

Need a quick way to tell Chip and Dale apart? Just remember that Chip has a small, black nose that looks a little like a chocolate "chip."

GADGET'S GO-COASTER

RIDE THIS MINI-ROLLER COASTER AND YOU'LL ENJOY THE HANDIWORK OF THAT CLEVER INVENTOR, GADGET.

QUEUE VIEWS

What is unique about the portrait of Gadget?

It's a postage stamp

What animals do you encounter as you ride Gadget's Go-Coaster?

Big green frogs. Watch out as you ride past them—you might get wet!

CHALLENGE!

WHO IS GADGET?

A member of Chip 'n' Dale's Rescue Rangers

TOMORROWLAND

IN TOMORROWLAND, SPACE EXPLORERS WILL DISCOVER SCIENTIFIC SURPRISES AND VISIONARY SECRETS THAT WILL CHALLENGE YOUR DISNEYLAND KNOW-HOW. LOOK FOR WHIRLING SPACESHIPS, ZOOMING ROCKET VEHICLES, EXPLORATORY SUBMARINES, AND KINETIC SCULPTURES AND FOUNTAINS—ALL BUILDING UPON WALT'S ORIGINAL VISION OF "A VISTA INTO A WORLD OF WONDROUS IDEAS," AND CHALLENGING FUTURISTS OF ALL AGES WITH EXCITING GLIMPSES BEYOND THE STARS TO A FUTURE FULL OF PROMISE AND HOPE.

THE FACT FILE

Tomorrowland is the home of Agrifuture: a landscaping design of blooming edible plants including oranges, lemons, and cabbages.

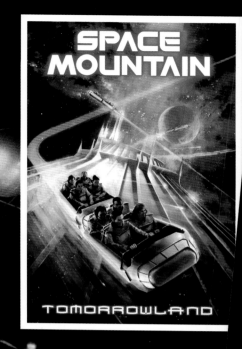

SPACE MOUNTAIN

TOMORROWLAND

SCAVENGER HUNT

Explore the "cosmos" by looking throughout Tomorrowland for pictures of planets and spaceships.

CHALLENGE!

WHEN TOMORROWLAND OPENED IN 1955, WHAT YEAR WAS IT SUPPOSED TO REPRESENT?

1986

STAR TOURS

ONE OF THE FIRST COLLABORATIONS BETWEEN THE WALT DISNEY COMPANY AND LUCASFILM LTD., STAR TOURS ALLOWS STAR WARS FANS TO ENTER THE ADVENTURE AND BLAST BEYOND THE STARS, THANKS TO THE SAME TYPE OF FLIGHT-SIMULATOR TECHNOLOGY USED BY MILITARY AND COMMERCIAL AIRLINES TO TRAIN PILOTS. STAR TOURS OPENED ON JANUARY 9, 1987, WITH A LINE OF EAGER STAR EXPLORERS SO LONG IT STRETCHED FROM TOMORROWLAND TO MAIN STREET'S TOWN SQUARE.

THE FACT FILE

The C-3PO and R2-D2 droids seen in the queue area are actual props from the Star Wars films.

EARS TO YOU

Actor Anthony Daniels reprises his original *Star Wars* role as the voice of protocol droid C-3PO.

Do you hear an announcement for Mr. Egroeg Sacul, asking him to see the Star Tours agent at gate number 3? Spell it backward and hear who it's really for.

There's another announcement for "Mr. Tom Morrow." This is a nod to the former Audio-Animatronics Mission Control Center director of Mission to Mars, a former attraction in Tomorrowland.

WHAT USED TO BE

Adventure Thru Inner Space, which opened in 1967, allowed guests to board Atomobiles and journey through the Mighty Microscope into a single snowflake as they were continually miniaturized. Inner space explorers continued to shrink "beyond the smallness of an atom" as they approached the atom's nucleus . . . and perhaps the point of no return. This futuristic attraction shrank its last adventurer in 1985.

STAR TOURS
From the Creative Forces of Disney & George Lucas

CHALLENGE!

WHAT IS THE NAME OF YOUR VEHICLE?
The Starspeeder 3000

LOOK OUT!

Look fast if you want to see a tribute to the Adventure Thru Inner Space as the Star Tours StarSpeeder races out of the hangar. On the bottom right of the screen, there's the Mighty Microscope, and its miniaturized Atomobiles.

WHAT IS THE NAME OF YOUR DROID PILOT?
RX-24, or Rex (Luckily for everyone, R2-D2 is also on board)

WHAT DOES THE PACKING TAPE LABEL ON YOUR STARSPEEDER DROID PILOT SAY?
"Remove Before Flight"

ASTRO ORBITOR

A "SPACE AGE" ROCKET ATTRACTION KNOWN AS ASTRO-JETS BLASTED OFF IN 1956 AND ORBITED OVER TOMORROWLAND UNTIL 1997. THIS MODERN VERSION—INSPIRED BY THE ORBITRON IN DISNEYLAND PARIS—SOARED TO NEW HEIGHTS STARTING IN 1998.

THE FACT FILE

There is an Astro Orbiter in Walt Disney World. Same attraction, different vowel!

CHALLENGE YOURSELF!

When you ride the Astro Orbiter, guide your rocket to its highest position. See how many Disneyland landmarks you can spy from your space-age vantage point.

Inspired by Disney•Pixar's TOY STORY 3

BUZZ LIGHTYEAR
ASTRO BLASTERS

BLAST OFF "TO INFINITY AND BEYOND" AS YOU JOIN BUZZ LIGHTYEAR IN AN INTERGALACTIC BATTLE AGAINST THE EVIL EMPEROR ZURG, IN ONE OF THE MOST INTERACTIVE DISNEYLAND ATTRACTIONS EVER. YOU CAN SPIN YOUR STAR CRUISER 360 DEGREES WHILE YOU FIRE MOVABLE, HANDHELD LASER CANNONS. AT THE END OF THE ADVENTURE, COMPARE YOUR HIGH SCORE WITH FELLOW SPACE RANGERS, OR GO FOR A PERSONAL BEST.

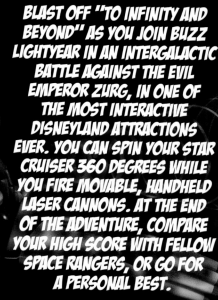

CHALLENGE YOURSELF!

Looking to rack up points? Aim your laser cannons at targets that are farther away or are moving.

Characters that are colored with blues and greens are "good," while those that feature reds and oranges are "bad." There are no targets on any of the good characters.

WHAT USED TO BE

Previous tenants included Circle-Vision 360 and Rocket Rods.

Amaze your friends and family by e-mailing your Astro Blaster score home directly from Tomorrowland.

EARS TO YOU

Listen up, Space Rangers, as you move through the queue area. Buzz Lightyear himself gives you vital instructions.

CHALLENGE!

WHAT KIND OF VEHICLE ARE YOU IN?

An XP-40

SPACE MOUNTAIN

WALT DISNEY DREAMED UP THE SPACE MOUNTAIN CONCEPT IN THE MID-1960S, BUT IT TOOK TWELVE YEARS FOR COMPUTER TECHNOLOGY TO CATCH UP TO HIS VISION. THE FIRST "INDOOR" ROLLER COASTER, SPACE MOUNTAIN TAKES VOYAGERS ON A GALACTIC FLIGHT PAST METEORS AND STARS, THE COSMIC VAPOR CURTAIN, AND THE SOLAR ENERGIZER. SPACE MOUNTAIN OPENED IN MAY 1977, AND WAS "RE-LAUNCHED" IN THE SUMMER OF 2005 WITH ALL-NEW SPACE EFFECTS.

THE FACT FILE

The first guests to experience the attraction were the first Americans in space—NASA's *Mercury* astronauts. When interviewed after the inaugural voyage through Space Mountain, one of the astronauts reported that it was "just like the real thing."

BY THE NUMBERS

The Space Mountain rockets have carried over 170 million Tomorrowland "astronauts," covering nearly 9 million miles —a distance equal to more than 18 round trips to the moon.

QUEUE VIEWS

In the ceiling of the queue area is a hatch labeled "Bay 12—Command Module Capt. J. Hench"—a tribute to Disney artist John Hench, one of the first Imagineers to draft concepts for Space Mountain.

ASK A CAST MEMBER

For the ultimate in space travel thrills, ask to be seated in the first seat of the vehicle.

SECOND TIME AROUND

During your high-speed space journey through the cosmos, count how many times in a row you turn right.

CHALLENGE!

WHAT IS THE CODE NUMBER OF THE SPACESHIP ABOVE THE SPACE MOUNTAIN BOARDING AREA?

Until 2002, the spaceship was marked DL2000 (DL standing for Disneyland 2000, meaning the future). With the dawn of the new millennium, the designation was changed to DL3000.

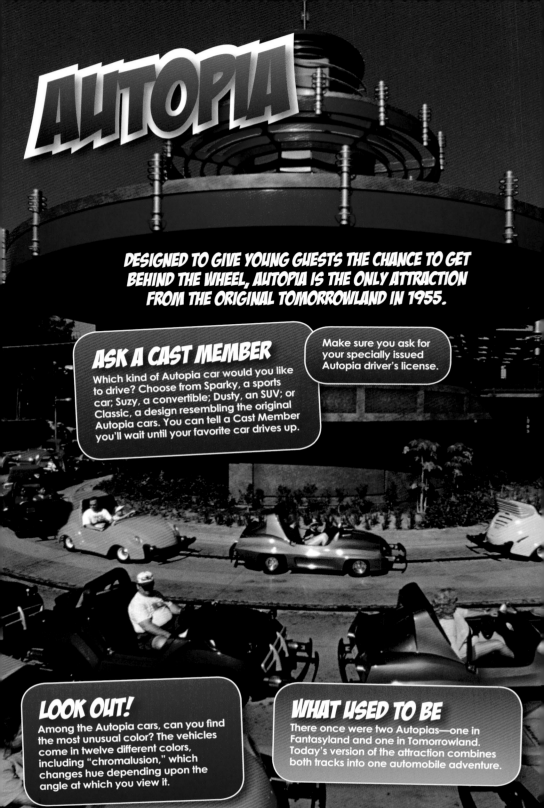

AUTOPIA

DESIGNED TO GIVE YOUNG GUESTS THE CHANCE TO GET BEHIND THE WHEEL, AUTOPIA IS THE ONLY ATTRACTION FROM THE ORIGINAL TOMORROWLAND IN 1955.

ASK A CAST MEMBER

Which kind of Autopia car would you like to drive? Choose from Sparky, a sports car; Suzy, a convertible; Dusty, an SUV; or Classic, a design resembling the original Autopia cars. You can tell a Cast Member you'll wait until your favorite car drives up.

Make sure you ask for your specially issued Autopia driver's license.

LOOK OUT!

Among the Autopia cars, can you find the most unusual color? The vehicles come in twelve different colors, including "chromalusion," which changes hue depending upon the angle at which you view it.

WHAT USED TO BE

There once were two Autopias—one in Fantasyland and one in Tomorrowland. Today's version of the attraction combines both tracks into one automobile adventure.

HONEY, I SHRUNK THE AUDIENCE

WHEN WACKY PROFESSOR WAYNE SZALINSKI DEMONSTRATES SOME OF HIS LATEST INVENTIONS, THINGS GO HAYWIRE, AND THE THEATER IS ACCIDENTALLY SHRUNK TO THE SIZE OF A SHOE BOX. THE MISADVENTURES INCLUDE A TOWERING TODDLER, A DINOSAUR-SIZE DOG, A MENACING VIPER—AND AN ARMY OF SKITTERING MICE!

CHECK IT OUT!

As part of the special effects experienced within this attraction, the floor of the theater rises four inches during the show.

CHALLENGE!

WHAT ARE THE SPECIAL 3-D GLASSES CALLED IN THIS ATTRACTION?

Protective goggles

INNOVENTIONS

THE FUTURE IS ALWAYS IN THE PROCESS OF BECOMING, SO THIS SPECTACULAR DISPLAY OF TECHNOLOGY SHOWCASES TOMORROW'S INVENTIONS AND INNOVATIONS TODAY.

WHAT USED TO BE

Installed in 1967, the Carousel Theater was first home to Walt Disney's Carousel of Progress. From 1974 to 1988, the theater was home to America Sings, a salute to American music through the decades. Fortunately, the critter characters from America Sings found a new home at Splash Mountain.

CHALLENGE!

WHO IS THE HOST FOR INNOVENTIONS?

Mr. Tom Morrow, the former Mission Control Center director of Mission to Mars

WHAT ARE SOME OF THE THEMATIC AREAS IN THE ATTRACTION?

Transportation, Health and Fitness, Home, Information, and Entertainment

FINDING NEMO SUBMARINE VOYAGE

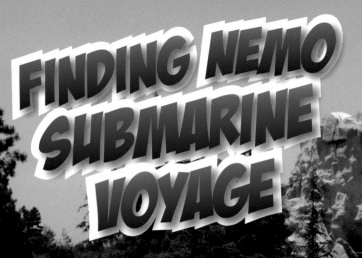

INSPIRED BY THE 1958 VOYAGE BENEATH THE NORTH POLE BY THE WORLD'S FIRST NUCLEAR-POWERED SUBMARINE, THE ORIGINAL SUBMARINE VOYAGE FIRST SET SAIL ON JUNE 6, 1959. WALT ENJOYED SAYING THAT THE DISNEYLAND FLEET WAS "THE EIGHTH LARGEST SUBMARINE FLEET IN THE WORLD."

SUBMARINE VOYAGE CLOSED IN 1998, BUT WHEN FINDING NEMO MADE A SPLASH IN MOVIE THEATERS IN 2003, IMAGINEERS KNEW THAT THE SUBMARINES AND NEMO AND HIS FRIENDS WERE A MATCH MADE IN DISNEYLAND.

CHECK IT OUT

Note that the subs are run by an organization known as the Nautical Exploration and Marine Observation Institute. Spell out the initials of the first four words (not counting "and").

If you are familiar with the original Submarine Voyage, watch and listen for some nods to the classic attraction throughout the new version. Look for a subtle but spectacular tribute to the silly sea serpent from the original toward the end of the voyage.

THE FACT FILE

Once powered by diesel fuel, the Disneyland submarines are now environmentally friendly electric vehicles.

The vibrant coral reef seen in the lagoon is "painted" with glass, in a technique that is much safer for the environment than actual paint. Over thirty tons of recycled glass, in over forty different colors, was used to add vivid, long-lasting pigments to the attraction's underwater world. Some of the unique-to-the-attraction colors are Mango Mud, Split Pea, and Aqua Jazz.

CHALLENGE!

CAN YOU NAME THE EIGHT MEMBERS OF THE WANNAHOCKALOOGIE CLUB?

Peach, Bloat, Gill, Gurgle, Bubbles, Deb, Jacques, and Nemo.

CAN YOU NAME ALL THE DEEP-SEA DENIZENS FROM FINDING NEMO YOU SEE ON YOUR SUBMARINE JOURNEY?

Nemo, Dory, Marlin, Mr. Ray, Bruce, Crush, Squirt, Chum, Tad, Sheldon, Pearl, and the Tank Gang.

FANTASMIC!

THE VIVID IMAGINATION OF MICKEY MOUSE BRINGS THE RIVERS OF AMERICA TO DAZZLING LIFE IN THIS NIGHTTIME SPECTACULAR. ONE OF THE MOST COMPLEX AND TECHNICALLY ADVANCED SHOWS EVER PRESENTED IN DISNEYLAND PARK, FANTASMIC! FEATURES A BATTLE OF GOOD AND EVIL, PLAYED OUT IN AN AMAZING DISPLAY OF PYROTECHNICS, LASERS, FIBER OPTICS, AND GIANT PROPS. THIS MUSICAL EXTRAVAGANZA HIGHLIGHTS SCENES FROM CLASSIC DISNEY ANIMATION WITH MAGNIFICENT FLOATING BARGES AND EFFECTS THAT WILL LEAVE YOU BREATHLESS!

CHECK IT OUT!

Special 70mm film sequences are projected onto three giant mist screens, each one 30 feet tall by 50 feet wide.

THE FACT FILE

Fantasmic! was originally going to be titled "Imagination" or "Phantasmagoria."

BY THE NUMBERS

Fantasmic! requires:

11	hydraulic or air lifts
11	watercraft
26	computers
101	cast and crew members
125	pieces of pyrotechnics

CHALLENGE!

CAN YOU NAME THE INFAMOUS DISNEY VILLAINS WHO APPEAR IN THIS NIGHTTIME SPECTACULAR?

Ursula, Chernabog, Maleficent, Kaa, Monstro the whale, the Evil Queen, and Captain Hook

THIS HUGELY POPULAR SHOW FEATURES SCENES FROM SEVERAL DISNEY ANIMATED CLASSICS. CAN YOU NAME SOME OF THEM?

Snow White and the Seven Dwarfs, Fantasia, Sleeping Beauty, Pinocchio, Dumbo, The Little Mermaid

WHO ARE THE THREE COUPLES WHO FLOAT BY YOU AS THEY SING AND DANCE?

Snow White and the Prince, Ariel and Eric, Beauty and the Beast

WHAT CREW APPEARS ON THE SAILING SHIP COLUMBIA?

The swashbuckling cast of Peter Pan

WHO PILOTS THE MARK TWAIN RIVERBOAT?

Steamboat Mickey

WHAT DOES MALEFICENT TURN INTO IN ORDER TO DO FIERY BATTLE WITH MICKEY?

A 45-foot tall fire-breathing dragon

A "BY THE NUMBERS" CHALLENGE

HOW MANY ATTRACTIONS DID DISNEYLAND HAVE ON OPENING DAY, JULY 17, 1955?

20

HOW MANY MILES OF MONORAIL TRACK ARE THERE?

2.5

HOW MANY GALLONS OF PAINT ARE USED EACH YEAR TO GIVE THE PARK A BETTER-THAN-NEW LOOK?

More than 5,000

HOW MANY "RIM LIGHTS" LINE THE BUILDINGS ON MAIN STREET, U.S.A.?

11,000

HOW MANY TOTAL LIGHTS ARE IN THE PARK ITSELF?

More than 100,000

HOW MANY MILES OF FIBER OPTICS ARE USED IN THE PARK?

350—more than half of which are in Peter Pan's Flight

HOW MANY SPECIES OF PLANTS ARE REPRESENTED IN DISNEYLAND?

More than 800 species of plants from more than 40 nations

HOW MANY ANNUAL PLANTS ARE PLANTED EACH YEAR?

Approximately 1 million

HOW MANY COSTUME PIECES ARE IN THE DISNEYLAND INVENTORY?

500,000

IN ONE YEAR, HOW MANY OF EACH OF THE FOLLOWING DO GUESTS CONSUME?

Hamburgers	4 million
Hot Dogs/Corn Dogs	1.6 million
French Fries	3.4 million orders
Popcorn	(more than 18.4 million gallons)
Ice Cream	43.7 million boxes
Soft Drinks	3.2 million servings
Churros	1.2 million gallons
	2.8 million

HOW MANY AUTOGRAPH BOOKS AND PENS HAVE BEEN SOLD IN DISNEYLAND SINCE 1955?

More than 16,000,000 autograph books and nearly 7,000,000 autograph pens

HOW MANY GUESTS HAVE PASSED THROUGH THE GATES OF DISNEYLAND SINCE OPENING DAY, JULY 17, 1955?

More than 500 million. The 400 millionth guest's name was Minnie!

DISNEY'S CALIFORNIA ADVENTURE PARK

CHECK IT OUT!

In the tradition of California's respect for the environment, Disneyland Park and Disney's California Adventure have Environmentality! In just one year, the Disneyland Resort recycles over 3 million pounds of cardboard, ½ million pounds of office paper, and nearly 10,000 pounds of aluminum cans.

LOOK OUT!

Celebrating the landmarks, lifestyles, and wildlife of the Golden State, a pair of 210-foot-long mosaic murals at the entrance feature spectacular Californian sights, such as snowcapped peaks, breaking waves, and majestic forests. Made of 12,000 hand-cast tiles, these colorful artworks take up a collective 10,600 square feet and are among the largest ceramic murals in the world.

THE GRANDEUR, STORIES, AND ENERGY OF CALIFORNIA OFFER EXCITING CHALLENGES INSPIRED BY THE RICHNESS AND BEAUTY OF THE GOLDEN STATE IN DISNEY'S CALIFORNIA ADVENTURE PARK. CALIFORNIA'S MAJESTIC LANDSCAPES, VIBRANT CULTURAL HISTORY, AND ELECTRIC LIFESTYLE ARE CELEBRATED IN FUN-FILLED ATTRACTIONS AND WONDROUS ADVENTURES THAT TAKE YOU TO PLACES IN THE PAST, THE PRESENT, THE FUTURE . . . AND THOSE ONLY FOUND IN THE IMAGINATION. THERE ARE FUN CHALLENGES AS DIVERSE AS THE LANDS YOU'LL DISCOVER: A THRILLING MOVIE-MAGIC TOWN STRAIGHT OUT OF HOLLYWOOD . . . A TREE-FILLED NATURAL ENVIRONMENT RESEMBLING A NATIONAL PARK . . . EVEN A MAN-MADE WATERFRONT COMPLETE WITH CRASHING WAVES. EXPLORING THIS CAPTIVATING SHOWCASE REVEALS SURPRISES AS DIVERSE AS THE STATE THAT INSPIRED IT.

CHALLENGE!

WHAT IS THE CALIFORNIA STATE ANIMAL? (LOOK FOR CALIFORNIA STATE FLAGS FOUND HERE AND THERE THROUGHOUT DISNEY'S CALIFORNIA ADVENTURE PARK.)

A grizzly bear (Ursus californicus)

THE ENTRYWAY IS A STYLIZED VERSION OF ONE OF THE MOST FAMOUS BRIDGES IN THE WORLD. CAN YOU NAME IT?

The Golden Gate Bridge in San Francisco

HOW TALL ARE EACH OF THE CALIFORNIA SIGN'S LETTERS?

11 ½ feet tall

CHALLENGE YOURSELF!
Have your picture taken posing in or by each letter in the "California" sign.

WHY DOES THE SIGN ON GREETINGS FROM CALIFORNIA FEATURE A POPPY?

The poppy is California's state flower

SUNSHINE PLAZA

SUNSHINE PLAZA REPRESENTS THE WELCOMING SPIRIT OF THE GOLDEN STATE. LUSHLY LANDSCAPED AND FEATURING A WALKWAY EMBEDDED WITH JEWEL-LIKE MOSAIC PIECES JUST LIKE THOSE MAKING UP THE VIBRANT MOSAICS NEAR THE GLISTENING SUN ICON, SUNSHINE PLAZA WELCOMES EVERY GUEST—WHATEVER STATE OR NATION THEY HAIL FROM—WITH A SUNSHINY FRIENDLINESS THAT IS DISTINCTLY CALIFORNIAN.

BY THE NUMBERS
Shaped like a wave, the perpetual fountain at the base of the sun icon is 9 feet tall and 52 feet long.

CHALLENGE!

THE FOUNTAIN AT THE BASE OF THE SUN ICON REPRESENTS THE DYNAMIC ENERGY OF WHAT OCEAN?

The Pacific Ocean.

SECOND TIME AROUND
Be sure to "catch some rays" at the sun icon at night, when the 50-foot-tall sun is lit by a dazzling array of red, orange, and yellow lights.

WHAT IS BAKER'S FIELD BAKERY NAMED FOR?

Bakersfield, the largest city in California's heartland.

DISNEY'S ELECTRICAL PARADE

THIS POPULAR PAGEANT WAS ORIGINALLY PRESENTED IN DISNEYLAND PARK. THE MAIN STREET ELECTRICAL PARADE WAS PERFORMED OVER 3,600 TIMES FOR MORE THAN 75 MILLION GUESTS DURING A 24-YEAR RUN, FROM JUNE 1972 TO NOVEMBER 1996. EVER SINCE JULY 2001, THE CAVALCADE HAS GLOWED ON AS DISNEY'S ELECTRICAL PARADE IN DISNEY'S CALIFORNIA ADVENTURE. MORE THAN 27 TONS OF BATTERIES POWER THE LIGHTS, AUDIO, AND FLOAT MOVEMENTS.

CHALLENGE!

THERE ARE MORE THAN 500,000 LIGHTS IN SIX COLORS. WHAT ARE THEY? (CLEAR DOESN'T COUNT!)

Amber, blue, chartreuse, green, pink, and red

GOLDEN STATE

THRILL SEEKERS WILL FIND EVERY CHALLENGE UNDER THE SUN IN THIS DIVERSE CELEBRATION OF THE LAND, THE HISTORY, AND THE PEOPLE OF CALIFORNIA. GOLDEN STATE HOLDS A RICH VEIN OF HIDDEN THEME PARK TREASURE. UNDER THE WATCHFUL EYE OF GRIZZLY PEAK, YOU'LL UNEARTH NUGGETS OF INFO ABOUT PROVINCES FROM THE DESERTS AND THE OCEAN, TO THE VALLEYS AND VINEYARDS, AND EVEN A MINIATURE WORLD POPULATED BY THE MOST ADORABLE BUGS ANYWHERE.

CHALLENGE!

NOTE THE WALKWAY KNOWN AS CALIFORNIA ROUTE 49. THIS SCENIC ROUTE LEADS YOU THROUGH WHAT PART OF THE GOLDEN STATE DISTRICT?

Grizzly Peak Recreation Area

GRIZZLY PEAK

TOWERING ABOVE GOLDEN STATE IS GRIZZLY PEAK MOUNTAIN. VISIBLE FROM ALMOST ANYWHERE IN THE PARK, GRIZZLY PEAK IS THE CENTRAL ICON OF DISNEY'S CALIFORNIA ADVENTURE.

THE FACT FILE

Grizzly Peak Mountain began as a 25' x 25' scale model, originally carved in foam. Laser scanners were then used to profile each piece of the model and translate them into full-size steel cages, which were lathed and carved as rock.

LOOK OUT!

Want a close-up view of Grizzly Peak? Use the special binoculars located at the entry to Grizzly Peak Recreation Area, just north of Condor Flats.

CHALLENGE!

HOW HIGH IS GRIZZLY PEAK?

110 feet

GRIZZLY PEAK RECREATION AREA

THE CENTER OF THE GOLDEN STATE DISTRICT, THIS ADVENTUROUS, ADRENALINE-INDUCING AREA PAYS HOMAGE TO THE NATURAL BEAUTY OF CALIFORNIA'S GREAT OUTDOORS, YOSEMITE-STYLE.

LOOK OUT!
You can spot old gold pans in the dry creek bed at the start of the Grizzly Peak Recreation Area.

REDWOOD CREEK CHALLENGE TRAIL

THE REDWOOD CREEK CHALLENGE TRAIL IS SET IN A LIVING FOREST OF YOUNG COASTAL REDWOODS AND INCENSE CEDAR COVERING MORE THAN TWO ACRES. A MAP POSTED AT THE ENTRANCE WILL LEAD YOU TO SUCH RUGGED ACTIVITIES AS THE TUNNEL TREE CRAWL-THRU, THE HOOT-N-HOLLER LOGS, PINE PERIL BRIDGE, AND CLIFF HANGER.

SCAVENGER HUNT

Follow the native animal tracks embedded in the walkway along the trail and you'll discover information on each species. Can you identify these California critters by their paw prints or other markings?

Bighorn sheep, black bear, porcupine, beaver, California quail, king snake, striped skunk, river otter, and mountain lion

Can you find rocks that are shaped like bears?

They can be found near Kenai's Spirit Cave

What symbols are drawn on the walls of Kenai's Spirit Cave?

Moose, buffalo, woolly mammoth, bear, hunters, and the sun

Around the Ahwanhee Camp Circle you'll find statues or totems of animals with Miwok legends. Can you find the hawk (or wek'-wek) and discover the legend of how it was born?

It's directly across from the Mt. Lassen Lookout Ranger Headquarters

Find The Millennium Tree, a real tree that was felled by a 1937 storm. The cross-section of the tree trunk is marked with California's historical dates.

It's near the trail's beginning after you walk through the giant sequoia tree archway

EARS TO YOU

Listen for Kenai's roar inside Kenai's Spirit Cave.

CHALLENGE!

NAME ALL THREE OF THE TOWERING LOG RANGER STATIONS.

Mt. Lassen Lookout, Mt. Shasta Lookout, and Mt. Whitney Lookout

WHAT IS THE NAME OF THE GIANT SEQUOIA TREE YOU CAN WALK THROUGH?

Big Sur

GRIZZLY RIVER RUN

BY THE NUMBERS

This adventure begins as the rafts "float up" the 300-foot-long ore trestle—20 feet higher than any other water-rafting ride. As rafters plunge over the final drop, falling 21 feet, the rafts spin 360 degrees.

Two hundred and fifty thousand gallons of water surge through Grizzly River Run. The beautifully sculpted rocks and boulders camouflage the necessary pumps and heavy equipment.

LOOK OUT!

Watch out for those pipes you'll pass under—they leak.

You can get splashed and soaked without even going on the attraction! Past the Grizzly River Run lockers is a path to the overlook for the final drop. The last section tends to get a good drenching every time a raft careens by.

EARS TO YOU

Listen for the rushing

GRIZZLY RIVER RUN IS INSPIRED BY THE BEAUTY OF A CALIFORNIA RIVER RUSHING THROUGH THE SCENIC FOOTHILLS OF THE SIERRA NEVADAS. DISNEY "LEGEND" TELLS OF A NORTHERN CALIFORNIA MINING OPERATION AT GRIZZLY PEAK, A RICH SOURCE OF GOLD. WHEN THE GOLD RAN OUT, A NEW ENTERPRISE SPRANG UP AROUND THE ABANDONED MINE—THE GRIZZLY PEAK RAFTING COMPANY, WHICH OPERATES THE GRIZZLY RIVER RUN. EACH RIDE THROUGH THE TALLEST, LONGEST, FASTEST RAPIDS ADVENTURE YET BUILT IS UNIQUE, BUT ONE THING'S FOR SURE—YOU WILL GET WET!

CHALLENGE!

WHAT DOES IT SAY ON THE PADDLE OF THE GIANT STATUE OF THE GRIZZLY AT THE ENTRANCE TO GRIZZLY RIVER RUN?

GRR (That stands for Grizzly River Run— and sounds like a grizzly's growl!)

WHAT IS THE MOTTO OF GRIZZLY RIVER RUN?

"The wetter, the better."

WHAT IS THE NAME OF THE FINAL DROP?

The Grizzly-Go-Round

CONDOR FLATS

CONDOR FLATS IS DESIGNED AS AN AIRFIELD IN TRIBUTE TO THE FLAT TERRAIN, BLUE SKIES, AND HOT THERMAL AIR CURRENTS THAT MADE CALIFORNIA'S HIGH DESERTS AN IDEAL LOCATION FOR PEERLESS PILOTS AND INNOVATIVE ENGINEERS FROM THE 1940S THROUGH THE MID-1960S. CONDOR FLATS MAY HAVE RETAINING WALLS MADE OF OLD RAILROAD TIES AND WORLD WAR II—ERA RUNWAY MATS, BUT FOR AVIATION FANS AND ADVENTURE LOVERS, CONDOR FLATS IS ANYTHING BUT A FLY-BY-NIGHT OPERATION.

SCAVENGER HUNT

How many times can you find the number 47 throughout Condor Flats? Look for the racing car in the Fly 'n' Buy shop, for starters. What's the significance of 47, you ask? The sound barrier was broken in 1947.

CHALLENGE YOURSELF!

If it's a warm day, hang out near the giant rocket jets at Condor Flats—and you'll get a refreshingly cool surprise.

SOARIN' OVER CALIFORNIA

THE FACT FILE

The building housing Soarin' Over California is themed as an abandoned World War II–era hangar, inspired by a similar structure at Edwards Air Force Base in the Mojave Desert.

Everything in the Soarin' Over California film was shot from a helicopter using a special IMAX camera.

SOARIN' OVER CALIFORNIA SHOWCASES THE BREATHTAKING NATURAL BEAUTY OF THE GOLDEN STATE IN A UNIQUE "FLYING THEATER."

CHECK IT OUT!

Watch carefully for an often-overlooked human detail in the scene portraying Yosemite. Six members of the Yosemite Mountaineering School are making their way along a cliff face before the famous waterfall comes into view.

All your senses are engaged in this spectacular attraction—you'll feel the wind in your hair and smell orange blossoms. You'll also smell pine, the sea, and sagebrush.

ASK A CAST MEMBER

Before you board, ask a Cast Member if you may sit in the attraction's front row. That's one of the most spectacular ways to experience Soarin' Over California!

CHALLENGE!

WHAT DISNEY CHARACTER MAKES A SURPRISE APPEARANCE AT THE END OF THE FILM?

Tinker Bell

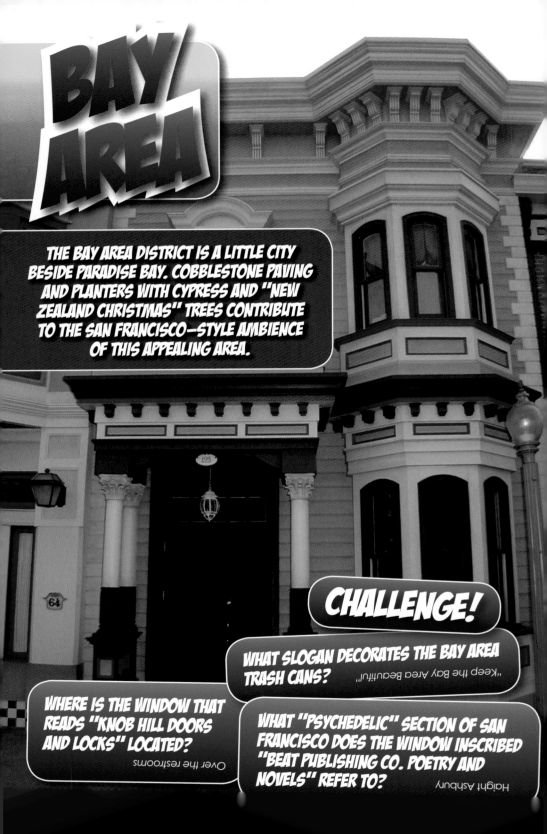

BAY AREA

THE BAY AREA DISTRICT IS A LITTLE CITY BESIDE PARADISE BAY. COBBLESTONE PAVING AND PLANTERS WITH CYPRESS AND "NEW ZEALAND CHRISTMAS" TREES CONTRIBUTE TO THE SAN FRANCISCO—STYLE AMBIENCE OF THIS APPEALING AREA.

CHALLENGE!

WHAT SLOGAN DECORATES THE BAY AREA TRASH CANS?

"Keep the Bay Area Beautiful"

WHERE IS THE WINDOW THAT READS "KNOB HILL DOORS AND LOCKS" LOCATED?

Over the restrooms

WHAT "PSYCHEDELIC" SECTION OF SAN FRANCISCO DOES THE WINDOW INSCRIBED "BEAT PUBLISHING CO. POETRY AND NOVELS" REFER TO?

Haight Ashbury

GOLDEN DREAMS

THIS FILM ADVENTURE IS HOSTED BY CALAFIA, THE QUEEN OF CALIFORNIA. CALAFIA WAS INITIALLY BROUGHT TO LIFE BY GARCI RODRIGUEZ ORDONEZ DE MONTALVO IN THE 1500S. THIS SPANISH WRITER ENVISIONED CALAFIA AS A WOMAN "MORE BEAUTIFUL THAN ALL THE REST, EAGER TO PERFORM GREAT DEEDS, VALIANT, AND SPIRITED."

THE FACT FILE

Eleven consultants, including historians, professors, authors, and librarians, participated in this show's development.

The home of *Golden Dreams* is a replica of the Palace of Fine Arts in San Francisco, built for the 1915 Panama-Pacific International Exposition.

CHALLENGE!

AS YOU ENTER THE THEATER, TAKE NOTICE OF THE STATUES ON EITHER SIDE OF THE SCREEN. HOW DO THEY BECOME PART OF THE SHOW?

The statues come to life and introduce the film

GOLDEN DREAMS COVERS MORE THAN A DOZEN DIFFERENT TIME PERIODS IN CALIFORNIA HISTORY. CAN YOU NAME SOME OF THEM?

Historical periods covered include the 1850s Gold Rush era, the Great Depression and the Golden Age of Hollywood (1930s), World War II, the post-war baby boom, and 1960s pop culture

PACIFIC WHARF

Modeled after Monterey's Cannery Row, this eclectic area celebrates the many diverse cultures that settled along the Northern California coastline. A hodgepodge of wood and brick buildings along the industrial waterfront, Pacific Wharf is also a tribute to the fishing industry, so you'll see plenty of netting and floats hanging along the pier.

SAY "BO-DEEN"

BOUDIN SOUR DOUGH FRENCH BREAD

SINCE 1849

THE BOUDIN BAKERY TOUR

The Boudin Bakery is in a Cannery Row—style factory building of weathered wood. At the end of the tour, enjoy a complimentary tasty sample!

CHALLENGE!

WHAT IS THE NAME OF THE LONG-HANDLED PADDLE USED TO REACH INTO THE OVEN?

It's called a "peel."

CAN YOU NAME THE ONLY INGREDIENTS IN BOUDIN SOURDOUGH BREAD?

Flour, salt, water, and mother dough

CHECK IT OUT!

The "mother dough," or sourdough, contains a natural leavening agent called *Lactobacillus sanfranciscensis*, which thrives only in San Francisco.

BY THE NUMBERS

Baking Boudin sourdough bread is a 72-hour process. The bread made here is used for the bread chowder bowls served throughout Disneyland Resort. The Boudin Bakery turns out 4,772 bread chowder bowls hourly, for a daily total of 14,536.

MISSION TORTILLA FACTORY TOUR

THE FASCINATING MISSION TORTILLA FACTORY TOUR ALLOWS YOU TO GET A TASTE OF CALIFORNIA HERITAGE AS YOU EXPERIENCE THE TORTILLA-MAKING PROCESS. PLUS YOU GET A VERY TASTY COMPLIMENTARY SAMPLE!

QUEUE VIEWS

Inside the attraction building's lobby be sure to peep through the small windows. What do you see?

Small holographic images of people making and enjoying tortillas.

mission TORTILLA FACTORY

CHECK IT OUT!

How fast are modern tortilla-making machines? They produce up to 1,200 tortillas per minute.

Want to know what your weight in tortillas is? Use the special scale just before the exit of the Mission Tortilla Factory Tour to find out.

WHAT DOES THE ELABORATE MACHINE KNOWN AS THE PROOFER DO?

It gives the tortilla dough time...

CHALLENGE!

HOW MANY TIMES DOES EACH TORTILLA PASS THROUGH THE OVEN?

Three times.

A BUG'S LAND

FLIK AND HIS INSECT FRIENDS WELCOME YOU TO A WORLD THAT'S BOUND TO DRIVE YOU "BUGGY!" IN THIS OUTSIZE LAND DESIGNED TO MAKE YOU FEEL AS SMALL AS A BUG, THERE ARE ACTIVITIES AND ATTRACTIONS INSPIRED BY THE 1998 DISNEY/PIXAR FILM *A BUG'S LIFE*.

LOOK OUT!

Near the fence outside a bug's land, there's a series of small signs with rhymed lines that lead you to the entryway. These signs are based on a once-popular advertising gimmick that used wooden roadside signs to display a humorous poem.

CHALLENGE!

WHERE CAN YOU FIND HEIMLICH THE HUNGRY CATERPILLAR?

At his Chew Chew Chew train in the (candy) cornfield, of course!

WHERE CAN YOU FIND THE GIANT BOX OF COWBOY CRUNCHIES CEREAL?

At the entrance to Flik's Fun Fair

BOUNTIFUL VALLEY FARM

A COLORFUL, INTERACTIVE LAND OF GOOD THINGS TO EAT, SEE, AND DO, BOUNTIFUL VALLEY FARM CELEBRATES CALIFORNIA'S AGRICULTURAL HISTORY IN WAYS THAT ARE POSITIVELY "EDU-LICIOUS." FRUIT AND NUT TREES, CITRUS GROVES, AND SEASONAL CROPS SURROUND THIS BEAUTIFULLY BOUNTIFUL AREA.

THE FACT FILE

California is the number one farming state in the nation.

LOOK OUT!

Look for sourdough bread in the shape of Mickey's head at the Farmer's Market.

CHALLENGE!

WHAT IS THE MOTTO OF THE IRRIGATION STATION?

"Things Grow Where Water Flows"

WHAT ARE THE TWO TYPES OF TRACTORS?

A crop tractor and a tilling tractor

WHERE CAN YOU FIND FOUR GIANT "SNAPSHOTS" OF FARMS, FIELDS, AND FARM EQUIPMENT?

On the wall to the right of the Flik's Fun Fair entrance

IT'S TOUGH TO BE A BUG!

Inspired by the Disney • Pixar film *A Bug's Life*, this creepy, crawly, experiential show combines an eye-popping 3-D film with in-theater special effects and audio-animatronics figures to reveal sensational—and sometimes slimy and slithery—secrets of the insect world.

BY THE NUMBERS
Bugs make up 80 percent of the animal kingdom.

QUEUE VIEWS
As you descend underground to the dark and mysterious cave theater, what do you see embedded in the pathway?

CHECK IT OUT!
Get ready to be "bugged" as the entire theater—including the floor and the seat in which you are sitting—seems to come alive with creepy crawlers of every kind!

Watch out as you near the entrance to *It's Tough to be a Bug!*—a much-bigger-than-bug-size figure of Hopper lurks nearby, and he looks hoppin' mad!

CHALLENGE!

WHAT INSECT SOUNDS DO YOU HEAR AS YOU WALK THROUGH THE QUEUE ON YOUR WAY TO THE THEATER?

Chirping crickets, buzzing bees, and mosquitoes are among the sounds heard

ONCE YOU HAVE DESCENDED UNDERGROUND, WHAT ARE THE LIGHT FIXTURES "SPROUTING" FROM THE QUEUE WALLS?

Glowing toadstools

FLIK'S FUN FAIR

THIS BUG'S-EYE-VIEW FESTIVAL LOOKS AS IF IT WAS DESIGNED BY THAT CREATIVE ANT INVENTOR, FLIK. EACH OF THE WHIMSICAL ACTIVITIES AND ATTRACTIONS IS "HOSTED" BY ONE OF FLIK'S MANY INSECT FRIENDS. AFTER MUCH "ANT"-ICIPATION, FLIK'S FUN FAIR OPENED ON OCTOBER 7, 2002, TO THE DELIGHT OF GUESTS OF ALL AGES (AND SIZES).

THE FACT FILE

The restrooms in Flik's Fun Fair are located in a 24-foot-high overturned tissue box.

CHALLENGE!

ACCORDING TO THE COWBOY CRUNCHIES BOX, WHAT IS THE CEREAL SHAPED LIKE?

Horseshoes

WHAT KIND OF BUG FORMS THE LAMPPOST LIGHTS SEEN THROUGHOUT FLIK'S FUN FAIR?

Fireflies

FLIK'S FLYERS

NO MATTER YOUR SIZE, YOU'LL BE BUG-EYED WITH WONDER AT THIS INVENTIVE "HOT-AIR BALLOON" RIDE CREATED BY FLIK THE RESOURCEFUL ANT.

WHAT DOES FLIK CALL HIS PASSENGERS?

Fabulous flyers

WHAT IS THE BRAND NAME ON THE GIANT RAISIN BOXES?

Fun in the Sun Raisins

CHALLENGE!

WHAT IS THE WAIT TIME SIGN SUPPOSEDLY MADE OF?

A button

WHAT SOUND EFFECT IS HEARD AS FLIK'S FLYERS LEAVE THE GROUND?

Whirring, cranking gears

TUCK & ROLL'S DRIVE 'EM BUGGIES

YOU NEVER KNOW WHO YOU MIGHT BUMP INTO IN P.T. FLEA'S CIRCUS TENT. THIS BUGGED-OUT ATTRACTION IS A (GENTLE) VERSION OF THE CARNIVAL FAVORITE, THE BUMPER CARS.

CHALLENGE YOURSELF!

Experience this attraction two different ways: as a driver and as a passenger.

CHALLENGE!

HOW CAN YOU TELL TUCK AND ROLL APART?

Tuck has one large eyebrow and Roll has two smaller eyebrows.

FRANCIS'S LADYBUG BOOGIE

AT FRANCIS'S LADYBUG BOOGIE, YOU CAN CREATE A NEW RECORD FOR A POLKA-DOTTY GOOD TIME!

THE FACT FILE

Ladybugs are better at detecting obstacles than humans, so the ladybug vehicles nimbly miss one another every time!

CHALLENGE!

WHAT IS THE SHAPE OF THE ATTRACTION'S DANCE FLOOR?

A figure eight

HEIMLICH'S CHEW CHEW TRAIN

RIDE ALONG WITH HUNGRY HEIMLICH AS HE CRAWLS ALONG IN SEARCH OF TASTY TREATS.

LOOK OUT!

Watch for large bites that have been taken out of many of the foods along the way. Can you tell that Heimlich has passed this way before?

CHALLENGE!

WHAT SCENTS DO YOU SMELL THROUGHOUT THE ATTRACTION?

Watermelon and animal crackers

PRINCESS DOT PUDDLE PARK

LOOK OUT!

Look out for the oversized hose nozzle with water that spurts randomly.

CHALLENGE YOURSELF!

Walk through this watery obstacle course without getting wet!

HERE IN LITTLE DOT'S COOL PLAY AREA, YOUNG GUESTS CAN MAKE A BIG SPLASH IN THE WATER THAT SEEMS TO BE EVERYWHERE—SO KEEP YOUR ANTENNAE UP!

HOLLYWOOD PICTURES BACKLOT

CHALLENGE YOURSELF!

As you walk down Hollywood Boulevard, tell the first person you see "No autographs, please."

CHECK IT OUT!

The towering movie studio gates that serve as the entrance to the Hollywood Pictures Backlot feature intricately carved elephants atop massive columns. This beckoning gateway is a tribute to the spectacular epics made throughout Hollywood history, especially pioneering director D. W. Griffith's 1916 film *Intolerance*.

STARGAZERS, GET READY FOR YOUR CLOSE-UP! YOUR CHALLENGE IN THIS LAND OF THE FUN AND FANTASY OF MOVIEMAKING IS TO UNCOVER THE LITTLE-KNOWN TRICKS OF THE TRADE AND DISCOVER CREATIVE DETAILS THAT PUT THE GLITTER IN TINSELTOWN. YOU'LL ENCOUNTER BEHIND-THE-SCENES DEMONSTRATIONS, FABULOUS SHOWS, AND EVEN A SUPERNATURAL ADVENTURE INTO THE TWILIGHT ZONE AS YOU RELIVE HOLLYWOOD'S GOLDEN AGE. A STAR'S-EYE VIEW OF MOVIE MADNESS AWAITS YOU IN THIS RE-CREATION OF THE ULTIMATE HOLLYWOOD MOVIE STUDIO.

CHECK IT OUT!

Notice how the asphalt has a shimmering, star-like sparkle.

LOOK OUT!

See the glitzy buildings at the end of the boulevard? Look again! It's a painting and some flat set pieces cleverly designed to look like a real street—just like in the movies!

MUPPET*VISION 3D

THE FACT FILE

Waldo the Spirit of 3D was so popular among the Muppet creators that the film team added him into more scenes.

LOOK OUT!

Muppet creator Jim Henson was a fan of "it's a small world." Can you find his tribute to that classic Disney park attraction in the show? (Hint: it's near the conclusion of the film.)

QUEUE VIEWS

The lobby is jam-packed with Muppet belongings. For example, there's a variety of bicycles, costumes, and theatrical trunks for Miss Piggy, Dr. Teeth and the Electric Mayhem, and even Sam the Eagle (in red, white, and blue, naturally). What else can you see? *Bombs, weights, and musical instruments are among the other props.*

SET IN A LAVISH THEATER REMINISCENT OF THE TELEVISION PLAYHOUSE ON *THE MUPPET SHOW* AND HOSTED BY KERMIT THE FROG, MUPPET*VISION 3D ENLIGHTENS GUESTS ABOUT THE ART AND ILLUSION OF THREE-DIMENSIONAL FILMMAKING—EVEN THOUGH THINGS DON'T GO AS PLANNED IN THE WACKY FX RESEARCH AND DEVELOPMENT LAB.

CHALLENGE!

WHAT SPECIAL ACCESSORY IS WORN BY STATLER AND WALDORF IN THE BALCONY OF THE MUPPET*VISION 3D THEATER?

They're wearing 3D glasses—just like you!

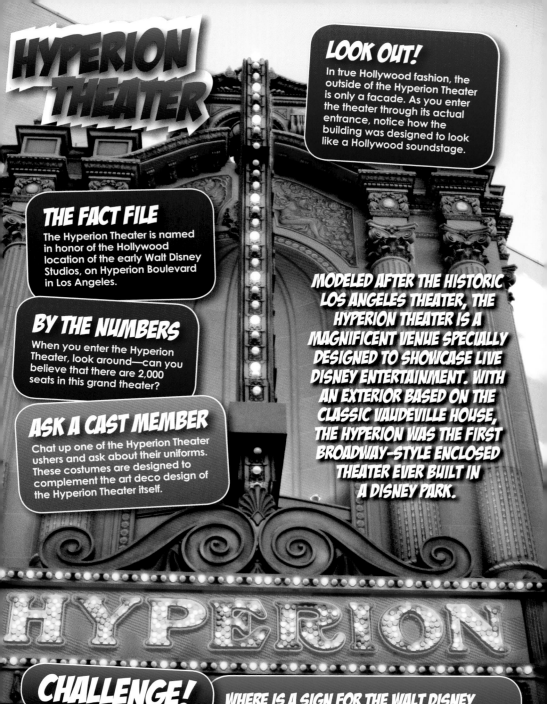

HYPERION THEATER

LOOK OUT!

In true Hollywood fashion, the outside of the Hyperion Theater is only a facade. As you enter the theater through its actual entrance, notice how the building was designed to look like a Hollywood soundstage.

THE FACT FILE

The Hyperion Theater is named in honor of the Hollywood location of the early Walt Disney Studios, on Hyperion Boulevard in Los Angeles.

BY THE NUMBERS

When you enter the Hyperion Theater, look around—can you believe that there are 2,000 seats in this grand theater?

ASK A CAST MEMBER

Chat up one of the Hyperion Theater ushers and ask about their uniforms. These costumes are designed to complement the art deco design of the Hyperion Theater itself.

MODELED AFTER THE HISTORIC LOS ANGELES THEATER, THE HYPERION THEATER IS A MAGNIFICENT VENUE SPECIALLY DESIGNED TO SHOWCASE LIVE DISNEY ENTERTAINMENT. WITH AN EXTERIOR BASED ON THE CLASSIC VAUDEVILLE HOUSE, THE HYPERION WAS THE FIRST BROADWAY-STYLE ENCLOSED THEATER EVER BUILT IN A DISNEY PARK.

CHALLENGE!

WHERE IS A SIGN FOR THE WALT DISNEY STUDIOS BASED ON THE BILLBOARD THAT STOOD ABOVE WALT'S 1930S HOLLYWOOD ANIMATION STUDIO ON HYPERION AVENUE?

Where else but right across from the Hyperion Theater!

MONSTERS, INC.
MIKE & SULLEY
TO THE RESCUE!

QUEUE VIEWS

Take heed of the "Attention All Monster Passengers" sign. Here are the rules posted there:

- "Those with tongues six feet or longer are not allowed to hang them out the window."
- "Gooey slime drippers and oozers are required to clean seat after use as a courtesy to the next passenger."
- "If you belch fire you are not allowed to sit directly behind the driver."

CHECK IT OUT!

Watch closely as you pass through the door vault—one of the doors appears different for each attraction vehicle.

Check out the headlines of the local newspapers, *The Daily Glob* and the *Monstropolis Horn*. Headlines include "Baby Born with Five Heads—Parents Thrilled" and "Scream Shortage Looms—Modern Kids Hard to Scare."

LOOK OUT!

Each of the taxi ride vehicles has a different license plate, including "MONSTRO," "FOBY AH," "SCREAMR," "GOTCHA," and "MNSTR4U."

RACE THROUGH DOORWAYS OF FUN IN THIS COLORFUL ATTRACTION INSPIRED BY THE DISNEY • PIXAR FILM, *MONSTERS, INC.* YOU'RE TREATED TO A WILD MONSTER'S-EYE SPIN AS MIKE AND SULLEY EMBARK ON A MAD SCRAMBLE TO RETURN BOO HOME, WHILE KEEPING HER SAFE FROM THE SNEAKY RANDALL BOGGS.

CHALLENGE!

WHAT IS THE NAME OF THE CITY WHERE THE MONSTERS LIVE?

Monstropolis

WHAT IS THE CAB COMPANY'S PHONE NUMBER?

555-FANG

WHICH OF THE MONSTERS, INC. CHARACTERS CAN YOU FIND ON THE FACADE OUTSIDE THE ATTRACTION?

Sulley, Mike, Bo, Randall Boggs, Roz, Needleman, Celia, George, and Smitty

WHAT DIFFERENT TYPES OF MONSTER SNACKS CAN YOU SPOT IN THE VENDING MACHINE? (EXAMPLE: A CAN OF PRIMORDIAL OOZE)

Other snacks include Sugar, Salt, & Fat; Bag O Calories; and Blort

AS YOUR TAXICAB ENTERS HARRYHAUSEN'S RESTAURANT, WHAT DO YOU SMELL?

Ginger and soy sauce

SECOND TIME AROUND

For some monstrous laughs, look carefully at the signs at the Monstropolis grocery.

Count fast! How many doors can you count on your ride through Monstropolis?

DISNEY ANIMATION

ONE OF HOLLYWOOD BOULEVARD'S MOST EXTRAVAGANT STRUCTURES, THE DISNEY ANIMATION PAVILION IS ONE ACRE OF ANIMATION. STYLED IN CLASSIC ART DECO DESIGN, THIS SPECTACULAR INTERACTIVE SHOWCASE CELEBRATES DISNEY'S MOST TREASURED ART FORM.

LOOK OUT!

On the real Hollywood Boulevard, you find stars on the pavement. Here you can find an image of an animation drawing—complete with animator's desk peg holes and some technical drawing instructions— embedded in the sidewalk.

COURTYARD GALLERY

Eleven giant projection screens and six large-scale screens bring to life the wide scope of animation through a variety of projected images. Some of the art seen here includes archival footage and still images that you may never have seen before.

CHARACTER CLOSE-UP

All sorts of animation art is displayed here, including visual development art showing the many changes a character goes through before the final version we end up knowing and loving.

LOOK OUT!

The hallway in this exhibitlike area is decorated with Disney characters, such as Timon and Pumbaa from *The Lion King*.

LOOK OUT!

On the Magic Mirror in the room of the same name, the signs of the zodiac have been rendered using familiar Disney characters. Can you name both the character and the sign the character represents? (For example, King Triton represents Aquarius.)

The others are: Sebastian/Cancer; Tweedledee and Tweedledum/Gemini; Phil from Hercules/Aries; Djali/Capricorn; Bull the Bulldog from Lady and the Tramp/Taurus; Simba/Leo; Robin Hood/Sagittarius; Snow White/Virgo; Fish from "The Nutcracker Suite" segment of Fantasia/Pisces; Lumiere/Libra; the Leviathan from Atlantis/Scorpio.

SORCERER'S WORKSHOP

This immersive experience enables you to interact, play, and explore the imaginative form of Disney animation.

CHALLENGE!

WHICH CHARACTERS HOST BEAST'S LIBRARY?

Lumiere and Cogsworth

TURTLE TALK WITH CRUSH

In this interactive encounter with the totally cool sea turtle, you'll have a chance to talk with Crush as he shares his awesome sea wisdom with big and little dudes.

CHALLENGE

ASK A STOR

THE TWILIGHT ZONE TOWER OF TERROR™

IN THIS SPINE-TINGLING ATTRACTION BASED ON THE CLASSIC TV SERIES, YOU'LL EXPLORE THE MYSTERIES OF THE ONCE-GLAMOROUS, AND NOW ABANDONED, LUXURY HOLLYWOOD TOWER HOTEL. CHECK IN AND DARE TO DISCOVER WHAT HAPPENED THAT FATEFUL NIGHT WHEN LIGHTNING STRUCK. THEN PLUNGE 13 STORIES INTO THE MOST THRILLING RECESSES OF THE TWILIGHT ZONE.

THE FACT FILE

The Twilight Zone Tower of Terror™ is the highest attraction in the Disneyland Resort, at 183 feet. So how is it that this attraction contains only 13 "floors?" Imagineers explain it's because the place is full of so many "tall stories!"

The elevators fall faster than the speed of gravity.

QUEUE VIEWS

Inside the lobby, how many clues do you see that indicate that The Hollywood Tower Hotel has remained untouched and undisturbed since 1939? For example, there's an unfinished postcard.

Other clues include 1939 magazines and newspapers left by hotel guests, two unfinished glasses of wine, and a deck of cards and a cribbage board left where guests were playing with them.

ASK A CAST MEMBER

There are actually three separate elevator shafts, each of which is subtly different from the others. Ask a Cast Member for a different elevator on your next trip.

CHECK IT OUT!

To create this attraction, Disney Imagineers watched each episode of the classic 1959–1964 TV series *The Twilight Zone*, created, hosted, and often written by Rod Serling.

LOOK OUT!

Be on the lookout for props and design elements throughout the attraction that pay tribute to specific episodes of *The Twilight Zone*. For example, in a display case outside the library, you can spot a broken stopwatch, recalling "A Kind of Stopwatch," an episode about a stopwatch that could stop time. And on the walls of the boiler room are chalk marks indicating a doorway into another dimension, as in the episode "Little Girl Lost."

The Twilight Zone episode introduction you see in the library was created using Rod Serling's opening to the episode entitled "It's a Good Life."

CHALLENGE!

WHAT IS THE HIGHEST FLOOR TO WHICH YOUR ELEVATOR RISES?

The 13th floor

WHAT IS THE NAME OF THE CLUB THAT WAS AT THE HOLLYWOOD TOWER HOTEL IN ITS HEYDAY?

The Tip Top Club (on the faded sign near the attraction)

PARADISE PIER

THE FACT FILE

The glistening Paradise Bay lagoon is four acres of beautiful California H_2O.

PARADISE PIER IS INSPIRED BY SOME OF CALIFORNIA'S MOST FAMOUS PARKS, SUCH AS LONG BEACH PIKE, SANTA CRUZ BOARDWALK, AND PACIFIC OCEAN PARK. AS YOU GET A BETWEEN-THE-EARS VIEW OF THE PARK WHILE SPEEDING ON A SOUPED-UP ROLLER COASTER OR FOLLOWING THE SUN ON A SPECTACULAR FERRIS WHEEL, LOOK FOR SURPRISES AND SECRETS THROUGHOUT THIS FESTIVE BEACHFRONT CRACKLING WITH SEASIDE SIZZLE.

CHALLENGE!

WHAT IS THE SLOGAN FOR PARADISE PIER? YOU'LL FIND THE ANSWER UP IN LIGHTS!

"Fun in the Sun for Everyone!" You'll find it below the Mickey head on California Screamin'.

AS YOU WALK THROUGH PARADISE PIER, SEE HOW MANY SEASIDE ORNAMENTATIONS (SUCH AS SEASHELLS, SURFBOARDS, OR DOLPHINS) YOU CAN FIND.

CALIFORNIA SCREAMIN'

BY THE NUMBERS

California Screamin' is 6,000 feet long and contains more than 36 miles of electrical wire and 167 miles of individual conductors.

Can you guess how high you go on California Screamin'? The first climb takes you up a steep incline to an altitude of 120 feet. Then what goes up must come down—you plunge 108 feet at a 50-degree angle at a speed reaching 55 miles per hour—making California Screamin' the longest, fastest roller coaster in Disneyland Resort.

The lagoon launch takes guests from 0 to 55 miles per hour in less than 5 seconds!

THE FACT FILE

California Screamin' includes one of the world's largest Mickey heads.

What do you think the California Screamin' attraction is mostly constructed of? Careful, this is a trick question! Though it looks like it's made of wood, this coaster is mostly steel, 5.8 million pounds worth. The majority of the steel is not necessary for support but was used to create the illusion that this is a vintage wooden roller coaster.

THE STEEL-STRUCTURE DESIGN FOR THE WOODEN ROLLER COASTER—
LOOK OF CALIFORNIA SCREAMIN' WAS INSPIRED BY SEASIDE RESORT
COASTERS BUILT DURING A THIRTY-YEAR PERIOD BEFORE THE GREAT
DEPRESSION. THIS ERA, FROM THE TURN OF THE 20TH CENTURY TO THE
END OF 1929, WAS KNOWN AS THE "GOLDEN AGE OF COASTERS."

EARS TO YOU

The rockin' onboard audio track was custom-arranged to match the twists, turns, and loops of the ride track—if you can even hear it with all the *screamin'*!

Scream tunnels are located in various places on the track to muffle the screams of riders zooming up, down, and around—so be sure to scream extra loud inside the tunnels.

SUN WHEEL

THIS CELESTIAL-FACED RIDE-WITHIN-A-RIDE WAS INSPIRED BY THE WONDER WHEEL AT CONEY ISLAND, BUILT IN 1927. WHILE NOT A COPY, THE SUN WHEEL INCORPORATES A CUTTING-EDGE, HIGH-TECH VERSION OF THE TWIN-RIDE CONCEPT.

LOOK OUT!

When viewing the Sun Wheel from across Paradise Bay, don't be so dazzled by the smiling sun face that you miss the illusion that its passengers seem to be boarding underwater. The attraction is set against the edge of Paradise Bay and loads passengers below the waterline.

THE FACT FILE

The Ferris wheel was named for G. W. G. Ferris, an American engineer who designed the first version of this classic ride in the late 19th century.

The Sun Wheel has twenty-four gondolas, sixteen of which slide on their own tracks.

SECOND TIME AROUND

Ride the Sun Wheel in one of the gondolas that is fixed on the perimeter. Then ride it again in one of the gondolas that move along the interior tracks during the ride.

CHALLENGE!

HOW TALL IS THE SUN WHEEL?

168 feet

WHAT IS WRITTEN ON EACH OF THE GONDOLAS?

"Paradise Pier"

WHAT ARE THE THREE COLORS THE GONDOLAS ARE PAINTED?

Blue, orange, and red

WHAT IMMENSE TOMORROWLAND LANDMARK IN DISNEYLAND PARK CAN YOU SEE WHILE RIDING THE SUN WHEEL?

Space Mountain

THE GOLDEN ZEPHYR

BLAST OFF! THESE SLEEKLY DESIGNED "SPINNING SPACESHIPS" TAKE YOU FOR A WILDLY RETRO SWING RIDE. YOU'LL HEAD FOR THE STARS UNTIL THE GOLDEN ZEPHYR SWINGS YOU BACK TO PARADISE PIER.

CHALLENGE!

HOW TALL IS THE GOLDEN ZEPHYR'S CENTRAL TOWER?

85 feet

SECOND TIME AROUND

Be sure to visit the Golden Zephyr after dark, when the gleaming attraction is illuminated by sparkling rim lights.

HOW DO THE GONDOLAS OF THE GOLDEN ZEPHYR "FLY?"

By centrifugal force

KING TRITON'S CAROUSEL

THE FACT FILE

The sea creatures on King Triton's Carousel represent aquatic life native to California, such as the Garibaldi fish, which is the state fish of California.

King Triton's Carousel was manufactured by the same company Walt Disney used to help him add horses to the King Arthur Carrousel in Disneyland Park.

CAROUSELS ARE THE HEART OF ANY BOARDWALK, AND KING TRITON'S CAROUSEL IS A QUINTESSENTIALLY CALIFORNIAN ONE, WHERE RIDERS ARE CARRIED ON HAND-PAINTED OCEAN CREATURES.

EARS TO YOU

1960s-style surf songs are heard on the classic band organ of King Triton's Carousel.

ORANGE STINGER

EARS TO YOU

While you spin through the Orange Stinger, what do you hear . . . and smell?

Buzzing bees and the scent of oranges

THE FACT FILE

Disneyland was built on the site of orange groves in . . . can you guess? Orange County!

CHALLENGE YOURSELF!

How many silly ways can you use the word "orange" in a sentence? For example: orange you glad you're at Disney's California Adventure today?

THIS TRIBUTE TO THE GOLDEN STATE'S PRODUCTION OF CITRUS AND HONEY IS HOUSED INSIDE AN A-PEEL-ING GIANT ORANGE RISING ALONG THE EDGE OF PARADISE PIER. BUZZ LIKE A BUMBLEBEE IN YOUR OWN SINGLE-SEAT SWING AS YOU SWARM AROUND IN FASTER AND FASTER CIRCLES.

GAMES OF THE BOARDWALK

THE OLD-FASHIONED MIDWAY GAME HAS BEEN MODERNIZED WITH A CONTEMPORARY FUN-IN-THE-SUN LOOK.

CHECK IT OUT!

Look for shop mirrors that comically distort reflections, fun-house style.

SCAVENGER HUNT

Which game is:

A play on the name of a famous Hollywood mountain pass?

Cowhuenga Pass (Cahuenga Pass in the Hollywood Hills)

A water-gun game using mechanical marine mammals?

Dolphin Derby

A basketball hoop shoot?

Shore Shot

MULHOLLAND MADNESS

MULHOLLAND MADNESS

THIS ZANY ATTRACTION IS INSPIRED BY THE FAMOUS ROAD THAT WINDS ITS WAY FROM HOLLYWOOD TO THE MALIBU COAST. THE ROLLER COASTER ITSELF IS KNOWN AS A "MOUSETRAP"-TYPE COASTER.

CHALLENGE!

AT WHAT POINT ON THE CALIFORNIA MAP DOES THE ATTRACTION BEGIN?

The Hollywood Hills

S.S. RUSTWORTHY

WHERE DOES THE NAME "RUSTWORTHY" COME FROM? ACCORDING TO DISNEY LEGEND, THE S.S. TRUSTWORTHY, A FIREBOAT FOR PARADISE PIER BAY, RAN AGROUND AND BROKE IN TWO—AND THE LETTER "T" FELL OFF THE BOAT—CREATING A WET AND WHIMSICAL PLAY AREA.

LOOK OUT!

Watch what happens at the S.S. Rustworthy every fifteen minutes!

CHALLENGE YOURSELF!

Play all the fun, interactive games the S.S. Rustworthy has to offer, including water cannons, bell ringing, lever pulling, and wheel turning.

MALIBOOMER

RAISING ITS PASSENGERS TO STARTLING NEW HEIGHTS, MALIBOOMER WAS INSPIRED BY THE LEGENDARY MIDWAY GAME CALLED THE "HIGH STRIKER," IN WHICH A WOULD-BE MUSCLEMAN SWUNG A MALLET TO TRY TO RING THE BELL AT THE TOP OF A TOWER. MALIBOOMER IS NAMED AFTER THE POPULAR CALIFORNIA BEACH TOWN OF MALIBU.

BY THE NUMBERS

It takes the Maliboomer less than four seconds to launch guests to the top of the tower.

CHALLENGE!

HOW HIGH IS THE MALIBOOMER?

Each of the three towers is 180 feet high

JUMPIN' JELLYFISH

YOUNG THRILL SEEKERS SIT IN FISH-SHAPED SEATS WITHIN BRIGHTLY COLORED JELLYFISH-SHAPED VEHICLES IN THIS FUN-IN-THE-AIR PARACHUTE ADVENTURE. ONCE GUESTS REACH THE TOP OF THE ATTRACTION, THE BELL OF THE JELLYFISH UNFOLDS AND ITS TENTACLES FLUTTER IN THE CALIFORNIA BREEZE AS IT FLOATS BACK DOWN.

CHALLENGE!

HOW HIGH IS EACH TOWER?

Fifty feet high

LOOK OUT!

Riding Jumpin' Jellyfish gives you that under-the-sea sensation—so be sure to look up and see the towering kelp garden at the top of the attraction.

DOWNTOWN DISNEY DISTRICT

CHECK IT OUT!

ESPN Zone, 36,000 square feet of sports-centered food and activities, boasts cutting-edge technology, such as satellite dishes and receivers, video cameras, and more than 165 video monitors—including more than a dozen in the bathrooms. ESPN Zone offers three individual yet integrated components: The Studio Grill, a restaurant recreating the electric atmosphere of the ESPN studios; the Screening Room, the ultimate place for guests to cheer on their favorite televised teams in a state-of-the-art setting; and the Sports Arena, offering sports fans a variety of interactive and competitive attractions.

STEPS AWAY FROM THE GATES OF DISNEYLAND AND DISNEY'S CALIFORNIA ADVENTURE PARKS IS A DAZZLING CENTER OF DINING, SHOPPING, AND HIGH-ENERGY ENTERTAINMENT. DOWNTOWN DISNEY DISTRICT IS AGLOW WITH ECLECTIC ARCHITECTURE SET IN A LUXURIANT LANDSCAPE. MANY DOWNTOWN DISNEY DISTRICT VENUES SERVE DOUBLE (AND TRIPLE) DUTY AS DINING AND DANCING—AND SOMETIMES SHOPPING—SPOTS.

CHALLENGE!

WHAT'S UNIQUE ABOUT THE LARGE BAS-RELIEF SCULPTURES ON THE ESPN ZONE STRUCTURE?

Their heads move

WHICH SPORTS ARE REPRESENTED BY THESE SCULPTURES?

Baseball, basketball, hockey, football, soccer, skateboarding, and women's soccer.

WHAT IS THE SHAPE OF THE FOUNTAIN AT THE CENTER OF PARADISE PLAZA, THE HOT, LIVE-MUSIC AREA?

A California poppy

WHAT IS MARCELINE'S CONFECTIONERY NAMED AFTER?

Marceline, Missouri—Walt Disney's boyhood home

THE DISNEYLAND RESORT HOTELS

THE DISNEYLAND HOTEL

LOCATED ON MAGIC WAY, THE DISNEYLAND HOTEL FEATURES FUN RESTAURANTS, THREE SWIMMING POOLS, AND A SANDY BEACH. THE ORIGINAL HOTEL OPENED IN 1955, THE SAME YEAR AS DISNEYLAND PARK.

CHALLENGE!

WHERE CAN YOU FIND STATUES OF MICKEY AND MINNIE AT THE DISNEYLAND HOTEL?

In the lobby, just inside the main entrance

THE FACT FILE

Near Goofy's Kitchen is a collage of Disney memorabilia, collectibles, and milestones, celebrating the history of Disneyland. The Photo Hall of Fame features members of royalty, political leaders, and celebrities who have visited the Disneyland Resort.

The Disneyland Hotel features a Peter Pan–inspired outdoor area with a swimming pool that incorporates a 100-foot waterslide, a pirate ship, and a comical sculpture of the Crocodile.

DISNEY'S GRAND CALIFORNIAN HOTEL & SPA

DESIGNED IN THE ARTS AND CRAFTS TRADITION OF THE EARLY 1900s, DISNEY'S GRAND CALIFORNIAN HOTEL IS THE FIRST-EVER HOTEL WITHIN A DISNEY PARK. RICH CEDAR AND REDWOOD PANELING DECORATES THE LOBBY, WHICH IS DESIGNED TO EVOKE A FOREST, WITH GIANT ARCHED TIMBER TRUSSES AS THE TREE "LIMBS." ITS GREAT HEARTH HAS A PERPETUALLY BURNING FIRE, AND THERE ARE POPPIES (THE STATE FLOWER) DEPICTED ON THE LOBBY'S MARBLE FLOOR.

CHECK IT OUT!

Visit the Storyteller's Café and check out the artwork on the walls, which represent stories set in the state of California. How many have you read?

DISNEY'S PARADISE PIER HOTEL

DISNEY'S PARADISE PIER HOTEL OFFERS SPECTACULAR VIEWS OF DISNEY'S CALIFORNIA ADVENTURE PARK. TWO HIGH-RISE TOWERS—ONE 15 STORIES, THE OTHER 14 STORIES—CREATE A CENTRAL ATRIUM, AND THE SUNNY FACADE COMPLEMENTS THE COMFORTABLE AND CASUAL STYLE OF THE PARK NEARBY.

CHECK IT OUT!

Mickey's famous silhouette is a part of the hotel's decor and can be found in the artwork, the ceramics, and even the upholstery.

CHALLENGE!

WHAT CHARACTER STANDS IN THE LOBBY AND WHAT IS HE CARRYING?

Goofy's "hanging eight," as he holds on to a surfboard

ANOTHER "BY THE NUMBERS" CHALLENGE!

About 2,000 items a month are turned in to the Lost and Found department. In addition to sunglasses and cameras, "finds" have included a TV set, false teeth, weights, and a waterbed. Still, Lost and Found has a fifty percent rate of returning "losts" to their owners.

The Mickey Mouse "Mouseka-ears" ear hats are the most popular Disneyland souvenir items of all time, with over 78 million caps sold since 1955—enough pairs of "ears" to outfit every American today under the age of 18.

More than one million plush Mickey Mouse toys have gone home with guests since 1955.

Disneyland has presented over 150 different parades since July 17, 1955. These festive processions have performed more than 25,000 times and traveled over 10,000 miles—enough to have crossed the United States twice.

THE CHALLENGE HERE IS FIGURING OUT WHY THIS INFORMATION EVEN EXISTS!

More than 17.5 million pounds of trash are collected and 3.1 million pounds of cardboard recycled by the Disneyland Resort each year.

Blue Ribbon Bakery on Main Street, U.S.A., sells enough coffee in one month to fill all the teacups in the Mad Tea Party attraction.

It's estimated that the Gibson Girl Ice Cream Parlor on Main Street, U.S.A., sells enough ice cream annually to build a full-size, edible replica of Matterhorn mountain.

Since Opening Day in 1955, Disneyland guests have eaten enough popcorn to almost fill the holds of two 600-foot seagoing navy transport tankers.